NOT QUITE PERFECT

TESS MACKAY

ISBN 978-0-6483144-8-6

Cover Design by Tess Mackay

Cover Image courtesy of BigStock.com

A NOTE FROM TESS

This book is set in Australia and is chock full of Aussie words and slang.

There's a glossary at the back, but if you have questions or need further explanation about anything in the story please contact me. I love hearing from you guys!

I hope you enjoy this book
love, Tess x

You can find Tess online here
Website: www.tessmackaybooks.com
Facebook: Facebook/TessMackayBooks
Instagram: Instagram.com/TessMackay

ABOUT THIS BOOK

How far would you go to get back your perfect life?

Victoria has the perfect life: looks, money, and marks. She's the popular kid everyone looks up to.

But it's all just a facade, if only people knew.

When a new girl, Vee, infiltrates Tori's friendships and takes over her life, Tori knows she has to do something. Not only is she losing her friends, but Vee's stolen the role of Beauty from her in the annual school production.

The only person she can turn to for help is Cole Black, who she's just found sleeping in her tree-house. Laidback Cole, with his surfboard and motor bike, seems to be the only person not under Vee's spell. No stranger to pushing the limits to get what he wants, Cole accepts the challenge to help Tori in her quest.

However, if her mother finds out the truth about the lead role mix-up, or the delectable bad boy in the back yard, all hell will break loose.

But maybe there's a way Tori can win back her friends

and keep her not quite #perfect life on her own terms. She just has to find it.

Perfection is over-rated. Or is it?

A sweet Australian YA romance served with drama and a delectable book boyfriend.

1 NEIGHBOUR

"Where is it?" I hold my hair out of my eyes with one hand, using the other to rummage through the duffle bag on the floor under the window. I should have unpacked properly last night. Now I'm running late, and I can't find my sketchbook.

Frustrated, I stand up and pull my hair back off my face and into a high ponytail. I use the hair tie from my wrist to secure it in place, then take a moment to breathe and find my Zen. Martha would laugh if she could see how stressed I was getting over something so minor. Then she'd tell me to learn from it and get myself organised next time.

Martha can go tie herself into a pretzel.

I loved her yoga classes while we were at my Gram's but Martha's lessons in mastering your inner Zen goddess haven't stuck. I'm trying, but without the regular dose of goddess goodness, I'm a lost cause.

A beeping noise outside catches my attention. A truck is reversing into the driveway of the house next door and there's a guy about my age directing it. From the back, he's cute. Black, curly hair drifts carelessly past his broad shoulders. He's cocky, he's wearing a sleeveless shirt to showcase his muscles.

Showoff. Although— his shoulders and biceps are worth showing off. My gaze drifts down to his denim-clad legs and boy, his arms aren't the only part of him worth showing off. I hope the face matches the rest of the package.

As if he feels my eyes on him, he spins around and looks up. I quickly take a step back.

My movement must have caught his attention and he stares intently at the window. Then his eyes meet mine. And he winks.

Oh my God. I groan and heat rushes to my face. I should have recognised the hair. It's Cole Black, aka 'bike boy'. His mother must have hated him to give him a name like that. We've got history, and it's not good. And a minute ago I was ogling him.

Get a grip, Tori.

There's no way he can be moving in next door to me.

No way.

He lives with his mum and I know they're broke. Or I thought they were. It's got me confused. Our neighbourhood is one of the most expensive suburbs. No-one rents around here; everyone owns their property and most of them don't even have a mortgage.

Not like us. Our mortgage is small, but we pretend it doesn't exist and we're just as good as all our snob hill neighbours. Which we totally are, even if our cars aren't upgraded every year.

So there's no way Cole Black can be moving in next door.

I step closer to the window and stand to the side so he can't see me. But he's not looking anymore. He's striding down the ramp at the back of the truck carrying a box. His mother follows with a rug, rolled up and awkward in her arms. The door of the truck swings open and a stocky man jumps down. He's in no rush to help. He leans against the truck and runs a hand through his slicked back hair, showcasing the sweat stained armpits of his white singlet. Ugh. I can almost smell the body odour from here.

Cole comes back outside and disappears into the truck, this time emerging with an armchair. He glances towards the man, who's pulled out a cigarette, his hand cupped around his mouth as he lights it.

Cole shakes his head and walks back into the house. He makes the chair look easy to carry, but I know it wouldn't be.

"Victoria, are you ready?" My mum's voice echoes up the stairs and I jump. It's the first day back at school and I'm not even dressed yet.

Mum must know. She only calls me Victoria when I'm in trouble, the rest of the time it's Tori.

It's days like this I'm glad we have a uniform at our school. I hate it, but I love it too. My face burns hotter as I realise Cole Black just saw me in my pyjamas. And not my cute slumber party PJs either. Just a ratty old T-shirt and a pair of sleep shorts.

Oh well. It's not like I care what he thinks. We're not mortal enemies or anything, but we'll never be besties.

I've known him my whole life and he's picked on me for half of it. I've always given it right back. But it's what he did in Year Seven, during the first week of our first year of high school, that stinks. In a way it was a good thing, it made me the person I am today. I decided that never again would I be the one they all laughed at and I reinvented myself.

I turned myself into one of the popular kids.

"Hurry up, Victoria. We've got to go." Mum's getting

serious now so I upend the duffle bag, spilling clothes, makeup, hair supplies and nail polish all over my bed in an untidy heap. I dig through the pile, but my sketchbook isn't there. My heart almost stops, and I suck in a deep breath. *Think. Where was the last place I saw it?*

I'm sure I put it in this bag. Pulling it closer, I begin to methodically go through the pockets. No luck. But then I feel a sharp corner at the bottom and realise there's something stuck under the hard plastic liner at the bottom of the bag. Hands clumsy, I pull the liner away and finally I breathe again. My sketchbook sits there, the golden cover sparkly like always. I grab it and hug it to my chest. Then I carefully open the bottom drawer of my desk and put it away, locking the drawer with the little key on my keychain. I know it won't stop anyone who really wants to get in, but it's a deterrent, and should be enough to keep my prying little sister out.

I dress rapidly, shove a couple of blank exercise books into my school bag, and run down the stairs. It's the first day back after the September holidays and it's not like we'll be doing anything except settling in. The teachers will talk about assignments and go over the curriculum for the term. It's going to be a long and boring day.

But at least I'll get to catch up with my friends. I'm pretty lucky. I've got the looks, the marks, and the money. And I'm the one my friends all look to for hair and fashion advice. They follow my lead, and I'm okay with that. Everything's perfect.

I'll never tell them the truth, that it's all an act. As far as the world is concerned, everything is exactly as it appears.

Yep, in Victoria Pearson's world, everything's perfect.

2 NEW GIRL

It's lunchtime and my friends have ditched me. Not exactly how I expected my first day back to go. I mean, I know I've been out of touch and we didn't get home until late last night, so I didn't even get to message them. But the holidays were only two weeks.

One of the drawbacks of my Gram's house is the total technology ban. Mum and Dad took away our phones when we left home and didn't give them back until this morning. We were in the car on the way to school, way too late, but if we'd argued we wouldn't have got them back at all.

Not that I can tell my friends that. Totally uncool.

Nope, officially there was no phone signal, and then my battery went flat. On all my devices. I didn't think anyone would buy it, but no-one seems to care. I've felt a bit out of the loop all day, to be honest. I expected Tiffany and Josephine to be waiting for me when I got to school this morning, but no. I was late, so I had to go straight to class, and I haven't seen either of them yet.

I spot Tiffany at our table in the lunchroom with the rest of our group and walk over. Josephine isn't there yet.

"Hey, Victoria!" Tiffany gets up and hugs me. I'm surprised by her use of my full name. Usually they all just call me *V*. "Where have you been? We thought you weren't coming back!"

Jo's suddenly there hugging me too. "How are you? When did you get back? Who have you got for maths? Did you hear about Cole Black?"

"Whoa! Slow down!" I shove into a seat beside Tiffany, making her move over. "I'm good. We didn't get back until late last night. We went up to my Gram's for the holidays, remember? Sheesh, it was only two weeks! No phone signal." I shrug. "What else? Oh, Mr Jetson. And what about Cole Black?"

Jo sits on the opposite side of the table and a blonde girl sits down beside her. A new girl? I frown. Since when did we adopt newbies?

Her long hair hangs smooth and straight down her back and my hand goes to my ponytail before I can help it. Everyone else has *their* hair out and straightened. Last term we all did the high pony. I'm starting to feel like an outsider amongst my own friends and my self confidence has taken a hit.

I fight back my frown. The first rule for being the trend-setter is to act like you don't care about what everyone else is doing. I've been doing that since Year Seven and they've all followed my lead. Except now they're not.

I study the new girl. Slim build. Pretty. She looks a lot like me with her blonde hair and pale skin. Jo turns to her and says something, whispering in her ear. I don't like how she's slotted in with my friends.

Then Jo turns to me again as if she hasn't been ignoring me. She's treating me exactly the way *I* usually treat outsiders. *What the hell?* We're supposed to be tight. The new girl is the one who's meant to feel like she's on the outside.

"I heard Cole Black's mother won Lotto or something. They're living it up and travelled first class to Bali." Jo's waving her hands around, animated.

"Yeah, he's not at school today. I wonder if he's even coming back," says Tiffany.

"Sarah Franks said they've bought a mansion and ditched the caravan park," Hillie Swan says from the other end of the table.

My heart sinks. They've bought a mansion alright. Right next-door to me.

"Hi, I'm Vee." The new girl grins at me and raises her left eyebrow slightly. "You must be Vickie."

I freeze, then give her all my attention, ice in my voice. "Pardon?"

Jo glares at me. "Be nice," she hisses. Then in a louder voice she introduces us.

"Victoria, meet Veronica." She giggles. "*V*, meet Vee."

"That's gonna get confusing." A voice drawls behind me. Josephine and Veronica are both staring over my shoulder, transfixed. Veronica's mouth is slightly open. I know why. I'd know that voice anywhere. Slowly, I turn and face him.

And glare.

Cole Black.

"I think *you're* gonna need a new nickname," he says. He leans down. "Neighbour," he whispers close to my ear. Then he straightens, turns and saunters away. He's all cool, calm and casual, leaving his hot, spicy, boy smell behind.

So good.

Damn him.

"Oh my God," says Veronica. She's practically drooling.

Her hand goes to her hair, smoothing the stick straight strands away from her face. "Who was that? And how do I get an introduction?"

I feel the sudden urge to punch her in the nose. First, she steals my friends. Then she steals my name. Now she's going to steal my guy as well? Not that he's my guy. But he's more mine than hers and she can't have him. I don't like this new girl. I know it's irrational, but I don't like her at all. But I can't let it show.

"I thought you said he wasn't at school." Jo nudges Tiffany.

"Guess I was wrong." Tiffany's gaze moves from me to Veronica, and there's something slightly shifty about it. "So, Vee," she says.

Veronica and I both turn to face her and I'm not sure who Tiffany's talking to. She shakes her head slowly. "One thing Cole was right about. It's going to be confusing calling you both Vee."

"I know!" Jo is bouncing in her seat, clearly excited. "Victoria can be Vickie from now on. And Veronica can be Vee. It just makes sense."

This can't be happening.

Seriously? I'm away for five minutes and some new chick comes in and takes my name?

My face is hot and my hands are trembling. I'm so angry I'm seconds away from punching something for real.

Someone. I grab the table and lean forward. "Not happening."

"It's not that big a deal." Jo's face is scrunched up and she shakes her head. "I mean, we can't exactly shorten Veronica, can we? And anyway, it's not like you own *Vee* or anything."

Veronica is sitting back, watching, a smirk on her face.

In fact, it looks like she's orchestrated this whole thing and is enjoying the show.

I push up from the table to stand. "I'm out of here. Tiff? Coming?"

"I think I'll hang here with the girls," says Tiffany.

My jaw drops, and I snap it shut. Up until five minutes ago everything was perfect, and Tiffany and Josephine were my best friends. I've heard other kids call them my 'minions', and sure, they copy my look and follow my lead, but it's natural that someone is the trend setter. Things have clearly changed over the spring break. My gut is telling me I've lost them.

"Fine." Pasting a smile on my face I turn to walk away. "See you later." I toss the words over my shoulder without turning back to see them ignore me. But as I reach the doorway I can't help it. I cast a quick look back at the table. No-one is paying me any attention except Veronica. Her eyes are on me and she has a sly smile on her face. She arches one eyebrow as if to say *I win this round*.

We'll see about that.

3 TORI, TORI

I stride through the door but stop after three or four steps.

Where exactly am I going?

It's a beautiful day and the sun is bright overhead. I know, I'll go and sit under the trees.

I walk in the direction of the bench on the far side of the quadrangle. I take deep breaths, trying to get my emotions under control.

Someone falls in step beside me and for a moment I think Tiffany has come to her senses and caught up with me. I glance over and snort. "You."

"Yep, me." Cole Black is walking beside me, his stride long and loping. He looks so relaxed and laidback, like he hasn't got a care in the world. He's wearing his sports uniform, but it might as well be boardshorts and a tee. A scruffy faded tee with an old surf logo on it. With his surfboard tucked under his arm.

I roll my eyes and fight a grin.

Way to let your imagination run wild.

"You okay?"

We've arrived at the bench and I sit, grateful for the shade. I wonder why Cole cares if I'm okay. He's not my friend, hasn't been for years.

"That was pretty brutal back there."

Great, he heard it all. "You know, we're not friends, Cole. Why are you following me?"

He laughs, and the sound twists my stomach in knots. "Someone's got to. You were looking a little lost after you made your big exit."

I felt lost too, but I'm not going to admit it.

"Besides. I've got a suggestion for your new name." He plonks himself on the bench beside me and nudges me with his shoulder. Like we're co-conspirators or best mates. "You're going to change your name, right?"

I scoff. "And let the new girl win? I don't think so."

"I saw them all at the beach over the holidays, you know," he says. "At first, I thought it was you, leading the gang like always. But then I realised it wasn't. She's taller, and never went in the water. Probably still too cold for her, but that wouldn't stop you."

"Great, so she's taller than me too." I shake my head, then think on what else he said. It's true, I love the water. Mum wouldn't let me get a surfboard so I taught myself to body surf. Nothing beats that rush when you catch a wave and ride it to shore.

But more and more I'm thinking that my gut feeling in the cafeteria, that I'd lost them, was right. Martha told me to listen to my gut in one of her Zen goddess lectures. "I'm not going to roll over and let the new girl take over my life."

"You've got to pick your battles, Tori, Tori." He bumps my shoulder again.

"Tori?"

"Yeah, Tori. You've always been Tori to me, from back

when we were little. It's only the last year or two you've been going by *V* at school. I always thought it sounded like you were up yourself."

My family calls me Tori too. But when Tiffany and Josephine started calling me *V*, short for Victoria, I just went with it. I thought it sounded cool. But it's only ever been at school.

"Yeah, I guess," I say. "Maybe it's time to go back to being plain old Tori again."

"Right, that's settled. Now you just need to bide your time before you take her down." He grins. "Let me know if you need any help with that."

"Thanks," I say. "But I think I'll be right. You've done enough."

"Glad I could help." Bouncing to his feet, quicksilver fast, he spins and looks down at me. "Now, you owe me."

"What!" The word sputters out. "Of course, you want something."

"It's all right. It's something you want, too."

I snort. "I doubt it." I glare up at him. "Come on, spit it out."

"Just, keep it to yourself that we're neighbours now. I don't want people to know where I live. Hell, I'm annoyed Mum went and picked the house right next to yours but she said she fell in love with the wooden floorboards and natural light, or some rubbish."

"It is a nice house." I've visited when the old couple lived there. "And you're right. I don't want people knowing we're neighbours, either."

"So, we're agreed?"

"Yep, agreed."

"Nice doing business with you." Cole dips his chin in acknowledgement. His gaze lingers, and he tilts his head to one side, assessing. "And Tori? There's nothing plain about you."

He's gone before I can respond, and to be honest I'm not sure what to say. *Did Cole Black just compliment me?*

What a weird day.

There's only five minutes until the bell and I spend it sitting in the shade mulling over his words. He's right, it's not worth fighting over the name *V*. I've always been Tori and it's time to reclaim it.

There's something else he's right about too. I've got to pick my battles. For now, I'm going to sit back and observe. Work out exactly how far the new girl has undermined me.

Then I'll come up with a plan.

4 INVISIBLE

I duck into the girls toilets on my way back inside. The bell's gone already, but I need a moment before I can face anyone else.

There's a girl standing at the mirror and she looks vaguely familiar. She's young. I remember that we have one of the local primary schools visiting today for their high school orientation day. Maybe she's someone's little sister.

I enter the stall, and when I come out she's still there. She ducks her head and won't look at me. She's trying to be invisible. Her face is blotchy like she's been crying.

Time to play the big sister role. I remember how scary high school was when I started. "Hey, are you alright?"

She nods but won't meet my eyes. I finally realise where I know her from.

"You're Jack Jones' sister, aren't you? Hadley? Hailey?"

"Hannah." She nods. "And you're Tori. I know your sister from dancing."

Jenna goes to a different school to Hannah but they're the same age and must go to the same dance academy.

"How's your day going?" I've decided to get her talking

while I figure out why she looks so upset. It might have been a mistake. Her bottom lip starts to tremble, and tears fill her eyes. She leans down and turns on the tap, so she can splash water on her face.

"Sorry." Her voice is wobbly. "It's not going well. I got lost and now I don't know where I'm supposed to be."

That's a problem I can solve. "I'm sure we can figure it out. This place is huge, and nobody expects you to be able to find your way around first go."

"I just want to go home. Look at me! I can't go back to class like this."

Alright, then. Not that I blame her. I'd want to go home too if I looked like I'd been crying.

"You're in luck," I say. "Give me five minutes and you'll be looking as good as new."

I rummage through my bag and pull out my emergency makeup kit. Hannah's eyes widen at the sight of it.

"I thought we weren't supposed to wear makeup."

'It's not makeup. It's an emergency repair kit." I grin. "It's a loophole."

I pull out supplies and get to work with concealer to hide the blotchy skin, and then blend in a light covering of base. A hint of liner around her eyes counteracts the redness. By the time I'm done she looks better than natural, and you can't tell she's wearing makeup at all. Exactly as it should be.

"That's amazing," Hannah says. "Can you teach me how to do that?"

"A good quality concealer and base, a light touch, and practice."

She doesn't look like she believes me. "How many years' practice?"

I smile. "We all start somewhere. Come on, let's get you back to class."

"You should do a makeup video," she says. "Like, step by step eyeliner for dummies. And concealer. I'd totally follow you."

"Maybe I will," I say. I could help poor kids like Hannah get a clue.

We swing past the office to get a late pass and work out where Hannah is supposed to be.

"Do you know Cassie?" Hannah asks. "She's Jack's girl-friend. I haven't seen her or Jack since this morning."

I wince. My pride is still hurt from what happened with Jack last term. I thought I liked him and went after him and lost. Big time. I made a fool of myself and was a total *biatch* into the bargain. I'll be surprised if Cassie or Jack ever talk to me again.

The worst part is, I didn't actually like Jack that much. Sure, he's hot. But I was trying to avoid the guy Mum wanted me to go out with, Trent, and thought that dating someone else was the solution.

Cassie and Jack are so cute together. They look like they're in love. I don't think I'll ever have that with anyone, it would mean opening myself up to get hurt and I'm not about that.

Hannah doesn't need to know all that, though.

"Yes, I know them. They're both in my drama class. We've got drama last period, so I'll let them know you're looking for them."

"Oh, no! Don't do that. I'm meeting Jack after school anyway. I don't want him to worry about me."

We've arrived at her classroom and I knock on the door and then open it. I deliver the note to the teacher and make sure Hannah has somewhere to sit before I leave.

"Thanks, Tori," says Hannah shyly. The name feels natural to me and I realise that Hannah would only know me as Tori, from my sister.

I smile and give her a little wave as I leave.

If only all problems were that easy to solve.

5 TRUST EXERCISE

By the time I get to drama class I've had enough for the day.

My friends haven't exactly been avoiding me, but they're not acting normally either. When I got to maths, late after helping Hannah, the only empty seat was in the front row. Tiffany was in that class and she usually saved me a back row seat beside her. But today she didn't. The new girl wasn't in the class, so that wasn't the problem. It was weird.

We walked together to drama after the class, but it felt awkward. We kept talking over the top of each other and then trailing off into nothing. Tiffany confirmed that Jack and Cassie are still together, but I already knew that from Hannah.

Our drama teacher is Miss Pretty. Seriously, that's her name. She's my favourite. We call all our teachers 'Sir' or 'Miss', even the married ones.

Miss calls the class to order. We're rowdy from being trapped in school all day after two weeks of school holiday freedom.

"We're going to do a trust exercise," she says.

There are groans from the whole class. Nobody likes these things and Miss gets us to do them *all* the time.

"Alright, settle down." Miss Pretty puts her hand in the air and we quieten. "You have to express yourself without words when you perform. The only way to do that is to tap into your emotions. Today we're going to do exactly that."

We all flick little glances to each other, like a hot potato. This sounds interesting but nobody wants to show their *feelings*.

"We've done physical trust exercises before, like where you fall back and trust your partners to catch you. This one is a little different." Miss smiles and gestures the floor around her in a circle. "Sit down so we can all see each other."

She sits, and the rest of us form a loose circle on the floor.

"This is a really simple exercise. I want you to share one thing about yourself that you consider embarrassing."

There's a chorus of *"no"*, and, *"but Miss"*, and many groans.

"Take a minute to think about it. Just something small." She holds up a hand. "And no nudity or other bodily functions."

This gets an uneasy laugh out of us.

"I'll start." She smiles and looks around the circle meeting each of our eyes. "When I was your age I wanted to be a rock star."

There's a mock gasp from around the room. Everyone's hamming it up, it's not really that shocking. But I want to know more.

"Now, you can leave it at that, a simple statement, or

you can expand on it. I'm going to expand because I can see you've all got questions."

There's a combination of eye rolls and nods from around the room.

"I played in a band and we thought we were good. We played lots of gigs around my home town and were going for the dream - rock stars." She makes jazz hands and laughs. "Then our lead singer got head hunted by a record company and the rest of us realised that he was the only reason we were getting gigs. We also realised we were just playing for fun, not stardom."

"Who was your lead singer, Miss? Is it anyone we know?" That's Scotty. He's always full of questions.

"You might have heard of him. He's got another band now. Catching Crows."

"No way, you know Eli Burns?"

"Wow!"

"That's unreal!"

She smiles. "Yes, Eli Burns is still a good friend. But it's embarrassing for me that I ever thought I was in his league. Even back then he was something special." She claps her hands together. "Now, who wants to go first? Remember, there's a cone of silence." She raises her arms above her head and mimes pulling the cone of silence down. "Nothing is to be repeated outside this room. And I know I can count on you to be supportive of each other."

Tiffany and Josephine are both in this class. So is the new girl, whose name I still can't bring myself to think. And Cole Black is here too. In fact, most of my group of friends do drama. And last, but not least, there's Jack Jones and Cassandra Parish.

Cassie raises her hand. "I'll go first," she says. Miss nods.

"I think you all know about my Instagram account, Cupcake4U?"

There's nods, and "yeahs", from around the room.

"What you don't know is the reason I kept it secret. I had a bad experience at my old school when I won a recording contract and the other kids thought someone else should've got it. They gave me a hard time. "

She looks around at each of us, meeting our eyes. Even mine. "In the end I decided not to pursue a singing career. But when I started my Instagram account I didn't want to be in the spotlight again. Then when I won the Pierre's Patisserie cooking contest last term I realised that not everyone is like those kids from my old school. You guys have all been really supportive." She trails off and looks down. "So, thank you."

"Thank you for sharing, Cassie," says Miss. "I want you to remember how you feel now. And how winning the first competition felt, compared to the second one. This is all powerful stuff and you can draw on those feelings when you're acting."

Miss looks around the circle. "Next?"

The girl sitting next to Cassie goes next, and one by one, everyone shares something personal and embarrassing. One boy, Angus, tells us he's jealous of his new baby brother. He knows he shouldn't be, but he can't help it. Miss says that you can't help your feelings, but you can control how you react to them. Acknowledging them is a great first step. And of course, use that experience when you're performing and need to show jealousy.

Tiffany is embarrassed that she's failing maths. Angus says he'll help her with it. Its cute.

Josephine is embarrassed because she says her face goes red whenever she *gets* embarrassed. Her face is bright red as she tells us this and we all laugh. With her, not at her.

"I'm embarrassed by my mother," says Cole. "But I don't want to expand on it."

"I hear you, man," says Scotty. "My mum's on Snapchat. She says she's keeping up with pop culture."

We all laugh.

"I write fan fiction." Jasmine, one of Cassie's friends, has a soft voice. She won't meet anyone's eye.

"That's really cool," I say. Some of the others nod.

Her boyfriend, Eli, is embarrassed at having to work in his parents' shop. It's a flower shop and he has to do the deliveries on weekends.

"But it's how Jasmine and I got together," he says. "She used to wait for me at her Grandmothers house when I'd come to deliver flowers. Every Saturday, for six months straight."

"I did not!" Jasmine ducks her head and looks like she wants to disappear into the floor.

"Yeah, you did," he says. He pulls her in for a side hug, dropping his arm quickly when Miss raises her eyebrow. "And I used to fight my brothers to be the one who got to do the delivery."

"That's so romantic," sighs Tiffany. It earns her a glare from Jasmine but most of us other girls are sighing right along with her.

When it's my turn I'm not really sure what to say. But everyone is being really open and honest, so I decide to do the same.

"I've got a sketchbook I would never show anyone. It's embarrassing," I say. "I'm not any good at drawing, but I enjoy it."

"It's good to explore your creative side," says Miss.

"There's a few of you who have creative hobbies. Writing, drawing, and playing an instrument are all good ways to express yourself. Thanks for sharing, Victoria."

"Tori," I say. I get a few weird looks and lift my chin. "What? It's my name."

There, it's official. It doesn't sit right with me, giving up my nick-name, Vee, to the new girl, but I don't have a choice. I need to pick my battles.

Cole gives me a nod. The corner of his mouth lifts in an almost smile. Maybe he's happy I used his idea and now he thinks I owe him again. Veronica smirks like she's won. She whispers something to Josephine. Something nasty, no doubt.

Miss notices. "Veronica, you're last one up. What would you like to share?"

"I've just moved to town and I was really embarrassed that I didn't know anyone," she says. Not exactly earthshattering. "But then I met Jo and some of the other girls during the holidays and now I've got friends, so I'm okay."

Miss smiles. "That's great. Thank you, Veronica. Now, class. I want you to remember how you felt today, being vulnerable and sharing something personal. Draw on this experience to help you express those emotions on stage. Think about how you felt inside. What was happening with your body? Did you get hot, or cold? Did your heart rate speed up? Or your throat get tight? All those physical sensations are attached to the emotions you feel and focusing on them can help you to be a better actor."

She stands and gestures for us to all do the same.

"I want you all to shake hands and acknowledge what you've just shared. And remember, what happens in drama class, stays in drama class. A cone of silence, guys."

I turn to Jasmine and shake her hand, then move on. It's

a blur of movement, handshakes, and the occasional hug. Cole grabs my hand at one point, engulfing it in his large, warm palm. He pulls me towards him and bends to say something in my ear. One word. "Tori." He pulls back and he's grinning like a Cheshire cat. My face burns: I don't know why. Then he releases my hand and moves on to Scotty, and they do the guy-shake, fist-bump, man-hug thing.

I turn to the person on my other side and come face to face with Veronica. She stretches out a cool hand for me to shake, as if she's offering me a gift. I take it and smile. I'll play nice.

"Tori," she says. Just one word, but so different to when Cole said it.

"Veronica," I say, and extract my hand from her grip. It's like pulling it out of a toffee vat, without the third-degree burns. She lets go slowly, making the whole process awkward. Which I guess is her intention.

Tiffany approaches and they giggle and shake hands, turning their backs on me. Tiffany is ignoring me, just like Jo did this morning. I catch Cole's eye from across the room. He shakes his head slightly and I roll my eyes. *It's fine, I don't need them.*

"Alright, class, listen up."

We stop milling around and turn to the front.

"Auditions for *Beauty and the Beast* are this Friday and the selection committee will make decisions over the week-end. On Monday we'll announce the roles. This performance is a big commitment, so only audition for a part if you know you can put the time in. There are roles behind the scenes as well as on stage. We'll need props, makeup and lighting, just to name a few. Each role will have understudies, but everyone has to pull their weight. Got it?"

"Got it, Miss."

"Yes, Miss."

"Woo Hoo!" This last from Scotty.

"Those auditioning for the acting roles, please choose a scene from the play for the character you want to play. You can use a piece you've already performed in class or do something new."

We've been studying the play the last two terms and performing various scenes. One of our assessment tasks was a monologue from *Beauty and the Beast*. So we all know it really well.

"There'll be a signup sheet where you can nominate your preferences. Those auditioning should nominate the role they want and put down a second choice and their preferred behind the scenes job. Everyone else has to work behind the scenes, so choose wisely. Questions?"

"Can anyone audition?" Veronica is asking. There's no way she can be ready in time.

"The acting roles are open to anyone studying drama as an elective. Preference will be given to Year Eleven seeing as this is the last year you lot get to participate. But yes, anyone can audition."

6 LEAD ROLE

I can't wait for Friday. The role of Beauty is *mine* and I've been working my butt off for the audition. It's practically all I did over the holidays. Without a phone or any other technology there wasn't a lot else to do at Gram's house.

I'm going to perform scene nine. It starts with Beauty writing in her diary and then the Beast comes in. He asks her if she finds him ugly. She can't lie and says she finds him difficult to look at, but she believes his heart is good. He says a monster. Her response is beautiful.

No, you're not a monster. Many people deserve that name more than you.

I prefer you, with your good heart, to those who hide an ugly heart behind a handsome face.

The main message of the play is that appearances can be deceiving. And of course, that love conquers everything. I love it.

In fact, the role of Beauty isn't as big a focus in the play as you'd think. The Merchant has more lines, and the brothers and sisters are key characters. And the Beast, of course. Whoever plays the Beast will have to be able to act out all the emotion the Beast feels. At one point at the start, when Beauty is distressed about her father leaving, Beast throws back his head and cries in *bestial grief*. The script says *Beast displays his bestial nature vocally with these types of bellowings throughout the play*.

I'm hoping Scotty gets the role. He'll be great to work with, and he'll have a lot of fun with it.

There's a knock on my bedroom door and I look up.

"How was your first day back?" Mum asks.

"Okay." There's no point going into all the nitty gritty detail with Mum, she won't understand.

"Did you see Trent Riordan?" Mum's voice is light and teasing but the meaning is unmistakable. I should have made an effort to see Trent Riordan. "His family went to Greece for the holidays."

I shake my head. "I didn't have a chance to catch up with him."

Mum would like nothing more than for Trent to be my boyfriend. He keeps asking me out and I keep saying no.

Not happening.

At least, if it does, it will be when I'm ready and not a moment before.

Mum drops it, thank goodness.

"I've booked you in for maths tutoring starting tomorrow." She's counting off on her fingers and tutoring is number one. "Acting classes start up again next week." That's two. "Your piano lesson will be tomorrow, too, straight after tutoring." And that's three.

I hold back my sigh. Here we go again, another term of perfection, coming right up.

"Pony club starts back on Saturday morning." Mum's

still listing things off on her fingers. "It will be an early start, so Jenna can be back in time for baseball."

"What about swimming? Do I have to do squad again this year?" I'm hoping she says no. Getting up at the crack of dawn to swim laps is nobody's idea of fun. I love the water, but the surf is my first choice.

"Of course. Unless you'd rather pick a different summer sport. Cricket perhaps? My friend, Ruth runs a girls' squad."

I shudder. "No, no, I'll stick to swimming."

"You should think about getting a part-time job, Tori. Maybe over the Christmas holidays. It will do you good to learn some financial responsibility and you can start saving to buy a car."

"I'll worry about that closer to Christmas." I like the idea of having my own money, but I'm already feeling exhausted thinking about all the extra-curricular activities I'm expected to do so that I can be *well rounded*.

"Or you could talk to your dance teacher and see if she needs an assistant."

"I'm not doing dance any more, remember? I'm in Year Eleven and need more time for homework."

Mum sighs. "I know. I think you could have kept it up if you'd just be more organised. But it could still be the perfect job for you."

She frowns, and her attention focuses on the sketchbook in my lap. "What are you doing now? Homework on the first day back?"

"No," I say. I pick up my script and casually lay it over the sketchbook. "We've got auditions on Friday so I'm going over my lines."

"Oh." Mum looks pleased. "You're going to be brilliant as Beauty. Do you want me to help you?"

I shake my head. "I've got it. Thanks anyway." I want her to go away and leave me alone.

"Alright then. Dinner's in half an hour. I'm ducking out to pick Jenna up from baseball practice."

I'm glad Mum didn't make me play baseball too. Ball sports and I don't mix. Jenna's got a similar after-school program to me, but she's still doing dance while I've switched to acting. We both do swim squad and pony club, and of course the piano lessons. Playing an instrument is essential to our education, apparently. And don't forget tutoring. Now I've only got maths but I'm sure that will change, depending on my report card. Reports are due home next week seeing as there was some computer glitch and they couldn't hand them out at the end of last term like they normally do. I can't wait.

I move the script to study the sketch I've got half finished. It's Beauty's dress, for the audition scene. It's going to be beautiful. And it should be ready for opening night.

Textiles and design is my favourite subject after drama, and my favourite part so far has been patternmaking. I've been working on the dress pattern in my sketchbook. I should be ready to cut the pieces and start sewing soon. My textiles teacher said I can use the school sewing machines at lunchtime. She encourages us to be creative and come up with our own projects. I might even be able to use it for my assessment task this term.

I glance out the window to the old fig tree in the back-yard. It's almost a full moon and the treehouse is outlined against the night sky. I smile. The treehouse is the best thing about our house. Jenna refuses to play in it now she's twelve and starting high school next year, so I've adopted it as my refuge. She doesn't realise how private it is. I hope she never figures it out, I like having my own space. I mean, sure, I've got my bedroom. But it's not the same.

Putting the sketchbook aside, I pick up the script and read through my scene one more time. I'll shut my door and act it out after dinner. I know I've got the part, I don't even really have to audition. Cassie might have given me a run for my money if we were doing a musical, but we're not. This is the traditional version of the play, not the Disney version. There will be dancing, but no singing. Which is just as well, singing is the one thing I don't do. I'm not a triple threat acting talent. Just the double, acting and dancing, thank you very much. And Cassie's got a great voice, but she's not an actor.

That's *my* talent.

I keep a low profile at school for the rest of the week. It's weird for me. I'm used to being the centre of attention and having Tiffany and Josephine follow me around.

Now that those two have adopted Veronica I find myself sitting back and observing more. I'm still hanging with them, and the rest of the group are treating me pretty much the same. But Veronica has stepped into the leadership role seamlessly.

The hair is the most noticeable change. Everyone is wearing their hair straight. Just like Veronica. Tuesday, I did the high ponytail again but by Wednesday I'd fallen into the mould and was wearing my hair out and straightened. I was mad at myself for caving, but if you can't beat them, join them. It's been years since I had to think about fitting in. I've been the trendsetter since our first year at high school. After the spelling bee debacle, I decided I'd never let myself be at the mercy of my peers again. I worked hard to be the popular one, the one everyone followed.

Now the tables have flipped and I'm having to think

about where I'll draw the line. The hair, I can do. I'm not sure what else I can stomach. But I know that high school without backup is a bad place to be, and I'm not willing to go back there.

If only I was more like Cassie and her friends. They don't care what other people think of them. Or if they do, they don't show it. Maybe that's the secret. Not showing it.

Finally, Friday rolls around. Audition day.

We've been allocated time slots throughout the day, a bit like job interviews. Miss Pretty organised it earlier in the week. We get two minutes to tell the panel what role we're auditioning for and why we should be the one they pick. Then we have five minutes to perform our scene. One of the teacher's aides is assisting, reading the lines of the other characters in the scene.

We have to wear our drama blacks, black leggings or shorts and a black T-shirt — the uniform for all our practical lessons.

The signup sheet at the back of the hall is for all the backstage jobs as well as the character roles. You can put down more than one option but it's Beauty or bust for me. I'm all in.

The hall is open so anyone can come and watch the auditions. There isn't a public vote, thank goodness. Seeing as the auditions go all day, and all the drama teachers and some of the English teachers are on the selection panel, the students from their classes will form the audience when we audition. That way anyone with stage fright will be weeded out. The teachers want to know that the people they pick will be able to perform on the night.

I arrive for my turn fifteen minutes early so I can watch the person before me. My time slot is just after lunch and I've been nervous all day with butterflies fluttering their fluttery wings in my stomach. It's good to have nerves, as long as you can channel them into the performance rather than freezing up. At least, that's what I've been telling myself.

Scanning the list of names already on the signup sheet, I pause when one catches my eye. Veronica Mooney. I study the list to see what she's put her name down for and frown. Not something backstage like I expected. No, she's going for the lead role, Beauty, just like me.

Well, I don't expect she'll be much competition. There's no way she's going to know the lines like I do. We've been studying this play all year and I've practised my scene until I know it backwards. *I've got this.*

The person on stage right now is Scotty and, as expected, he's auditioning for the Beast. He's brilliant. There isn't anyone else in our year who'll be able to compete with him. Nope, Scotty *is* the Beast. I smile. I'm looking forward to acting with him. We'll have a lot of fun.

"Hey, Tori, Tori."

I look around to see Cole. He's smirking, as if at an inside joke, and I feel my face heat up. I'm not a self-conscious person, but I'd feel better if he wasn't watching me.

"You hanging around?" I ask.

"Yep, your own personal cheer squad." His voice is light.

"Great. Well, I better go and get my head on straight."

Cole shoves his hands deep in his pockets, slouching against the wall. He's not going anywhere. "Break a leg."

The smirk lingers on his face and I ignore it. I don't have the head space to figure out what's going on with Cole.

I walk up to the side of the stage and take a seat in one of the chairs set aside for auditionees. I'm on my own, and a few students in the front rows glance at me. Everyone else has their eyes glued to Scotty. He's wrapping up his scene with one of those *bestial bellows*. He's nailed it. He'll be a tough act to follow, but I'm ready.

There's a smattering of applause and a few wolf whistles when Scotty finishes. Then it's my turn.

8 MY TURN

I wasn't at all nervous, except for those light butterfly flutters, until I walked onto the stage. All of a sudden I've got a bad feeling about this audition. My stomach is churning and I'm light headed. Nerves on overdrive, butterflies in full flight. I hand my scene to the teacher's aide who'll be helping and move front and centre to face the judging panel.

"Victoria," says Miss Pretty. "Please tell us what role you're auditioning for and why you should be the one we choose."

"Good afternoon, judges." I take a deep breath before continuing. The dramatic pause. Presentation is everything, my mother says.

"I'm Tori, and I'm auditioning for the role of Beauty," I say. "I was born for this role. It was made for me. I *am* Beauty." I put emphasis on the 'am'. A lot of emphasis. I almost hear an echo.

There's complete silence. No feedback at all. The butterflies are trying to escape from my belly and my palms are sweaty. Shouldn't they be smiling, or nodding, or something?

"I mean, look at me, right?" I gesture the length of my body with a dramatic wave of my hand.

Nothing. There's no reaction. I laugh lightly, hoping to portray that I meant it as a joke. And maybe get someone to join in. I expected at least a few laughs from the audience but it's a tough crowd.

One of the judges turns to the one next to her and whispers something. I glance at Cole, lounging against the wall at the back. He's shaking his head and grinning. See, he thought it was funny. Alright, moving on.

"The scene I'll be performing is scene nine."

"When you're ready," says Miss Pretty.

I turn to the teacher's aide and nod for him to start.

Then I launch my performance into high gear. I put my heart and soul into it, but it feels hollow. I remember all my lines, in fact I don't miss a beat. But something is missing. The flat joke has thrown me, and I panic. This has never happened to me before. I need to ramp it up even more. I need to nail the last line.

There's only one thing that could make it worse, and that's if Veronica was watching. And of course, there she is, sitting at the side of the stage waiting for her turn. All of her attention is on me, and when she catches my eye, she lifts an eyebrow. I refuse to be distracted.

"Tell me, Beauty. Am I ugly to you?" says the teacher's aide.

I fling my arms to the side and take two steps away. Then I whirl around and stride back to the Beast, speaking passionately. This is it. This is the line I've been waiting for. I put everything into it. Eyes flashing, gesturing big with my hands and arms, I practically throw my whole body into it.

"No, you're not a monster! Many people deserve that name more than you. I prefer you, with your good heart, to those who hide an ugly heart behind a handsome face!"

Oh boy. That was too much. One of the judges, Mrs Smythe the English teacher, is shaking her head.

I realise the aide has gone silent and I just missed my cue. "Yes, Beast," I say hurriedly. I've only got, like, two more lines and this scene is over and I can escape.

"Will you marry me, Beauty?"

"No, I will not."

I've blown it. I've totally blown it. There's no way the judges will pick me. Unless, by some miracle, nobody else does a better job. I mean, they know I've got the goods. Everyone has a bad audition every now and again. It will be okay. I've just got to get through my last line.

The teacher's aide has been droning on for a while and I tune in to hear him say, "Do I have your leave to go?"

I focus. "Yes, of course."

And three, two, one for the dramatic pause.

Take a bow.

It's over.

Cue dead silence. And my teacher clearing her throat.

"Thank you, Tori," says Miss Pretty. "We'll be letting everyone know who we cast on Monday."

I nod numbly and walk off stage and down the stairs. I pass Veronica at the bottom. She reaches out a hand to stop me.

"That was an interesting interpretation of the scene," she says. "Are you going to hang around to see how I do it?"

No way. She's doing the same scene?

I nod, but don't trust my voice. My throat is thick with unshed tears. I've got to hold onto the hope that even though I was *slightly* over-enthusiastic I'm still the best person for Beauty. I meant what I said earlier. I *am* Beauty.

I flick my gaze over to Cole, still lounging at the back of the hall. I've even got my own Beast. I scoff, thinking about how the story ends. There's no way he's a prince under all his bad boy colours.

Is there?

Veronica steps onto the stage like she owns it. She addresses the judges confidently.

"Thank you for letting me audition even though I'm new to this school," she says. So polite. "I'd like to audition for the role of Beauty. I love *Beauty and the Beast* and I think it would help me settle in and make friends if I'm involved in the play." She puts her hands together in the '*namaste*' position and does a little bow.

I roll my eyes. She's really laying it on. And she's not finished.

"We did this play at my old school and I was lucky enough to be Beauty." She looks away as if she's embarrassed and then peeks up from under her fluttering eyelashes. "People said I was good, not that I can take credit. Our drama teacher was Sebastian Blake."

Damn, that's bad news for me. Sebastian Blake is a well-known drama teacher and he's famous for picking unknown actors in his plays, who then go on to become big household names. The teachers are whispering excitedly to each other. That can't be good.

"I'm performing the same scene as the last girl, scene nine."

My heart sinks. This *really* isn't good.

Veronica nods to the teacher's aide and they begin.

She does it totally differently to me.

I feel cold all over. I've got goosebumps from this performance. Veronica is hitting all the notes I didn't. The something that was missing from my performance is present in hers, in spades. I feel hollow. Deep down, I know. Veronica is Beauty, not me.

She finally gets to the big finish. Those lines I love, the ones I thought I'd nailed. And her performance is everything that mine was not. She plays it low key, soft and slow. That line, the one about preferring Beast with his good heart, she almost whispers. I find myself leaning in to hear her. And it's not just me who's drawn in. Everyone in the hall is doing the same. Everyone. She's brought every single emotion that I felt I was missing.

She's brilliant. Epic, even.

I did it all wrong. And I've made a complete fool of myself.

9 RUN AWAY

I power walk out of that hall like something is chasing me. I fight back tears and when Cole tries to bail me up I ignore him.

"Tori, wait!" Cole isn't taking no for an answer. His long legs quickly catch up to me. "Are you okay?"

I shake my head mutely. My throat has closed up and I can't talk. I walk faster, if that's even possible. I don't know where I'm going, I just walk.

"Want to run away with me?"

That stops me. I turn to face Cole. His eyes are gleaming like he's got the secret to life and he's about to share it with me. I'm being drawn in against my will. "What did you say?"

"Come with me, Tori. Run away with me."

I shake my head slowly, confused. "You're not making sense. Why would I go anywhere with you?"

His face falls and he looks away. He's seconds away from storming off, I can see his muscles tensing.

I immediately feel bad. I can see how that must have sounded. He was trying to do something nice for me and

I've hurt his feelings. "I'm sorry. I didn't mean it like that, you just confused me. And right now, all I want to do is hide under a rock and ignore everyone."

Slowly, he unclenches his fist. "That's where I can help you." He raises his head and meets my eyes. "I'm ditching, Tori. I'm thought you might like to hit the beach with me."

My eyes widen. "I've never ditched school."

"I don't have all day. You coming or what?"

"My mum will kill me."

"She doesn't have to know."

"Of course, she'll know. We can't exactly leave by the front gate without being seen. And the teachers will notice if I'm not in class."

Cole looks at me as if I'm stupid. "There's auditions in the hall all afternoon. No-one cares if we're in class or not. And we're not leaving by the front gate."

He grabs my hand and starts walking. "Come on."

I let myself be dragged along, my school bag dangling off my shoulder. He's right about class. If they notice I'm not there, they'll assume I'm at the hall watching the auditions. My mother will never know. And I really need to get out of here.

The thought crosses my mind that Cole is the only person who has bothered to check on me. None of my so-called friends even called out to me as I left the hall. I saw them, Tiffany and Jo. They were in the audience watching the whole thing. My audition. Then Veronica's.

I frown. They should have followed me out of the hall. Why didn't they? Too busy congratulating Veronica, I bet.

Cole has taken several dizzying turns through the corridors and I clutch his hand grimly. When we burst outside I throw my arm up to shield my eyes. Too bright.

"Here."

Something is thrust into my hand, something smooth and hard. His sunglasses. I put them on gratefully. "Thanks."

He doesn't say anything else, just grabs my hand again and starts walking. We slip behind the science labs and head towards the fence. It's close to the building here and the angle we're taking is carefully planned. No-one can see us from the windows. It's a blind spot.

We're really doing this. I'm ditching school. My stomach twists as a surge of adrenaline hits me. I pull on Cole's hand. "Wait!"

"What?" He stops but doesn't let go.

"I can't go. I have to—" I trail off.

"You can do this." He puts his free hand on my shoulder and bends close. I get a whiff of hot, spicy boy and lean in before I can catch myself. "You know you want to."

I take a deep breath, inadvertently catching more of that tantalising smell. I let it out, slowly. You only live once, and I can't be at school any longer, not after my humiliation. I nod decisively. "Okay. Let's go."

He grins his wicked, cocky grin, and I bask in his approval.

"This is the tricky bit. There's a gap in the fence near that fence post. See how there's two posts close together? We can squeeze through there."

There doesn't look like there's a gap to me. "Are you sure?"

"Have a little faith." He's solemn now. "But we've got to move fast. You ready?"

I nod and he drops his hand from my shoulder. "Let's go!"

Cole runs, taking me with him. I feel like I'm flying and realise he's got my school bag. No wonder I feel lighter.

We reach the fence and he throws both our bags over. "Now we've got to go." The wicked grin is back. He pushes on one of the fence posts and it leans away from the other one, creating a gap. Cole steps through and pulls me after him. It's a tight fit and I feel like I'm getting squashed.

"I'm stuck."

Cole pushes harder on the post and yanks on my hand, hard. I twist sideways and pop through the fence, tumbling to the ground.

"Sorry about that." He's pushing the fence post back into place and you can hardly tell there's a gap. He extends his hand and I take it and am hauled to my feet.

Cole scoops up our bags and hurries me away from the fence into the bush a few metres away. He doesn't let go of my hand.

"We did it!" Jubilation fills me, and I want to scream with joy. We're pushing through the scrub, branches flying past our faces and scratching at our legs. Something sharp stings my leg.

"Ouch!" I glance down but can't see what got me.

Cole is still weaving through the trees. I'm close behind and slam into his back as he comes to a stop. We've burst out of the dense scrub onto a sandy path, almost trampling a woman walking her dog. She gives us a dirty look. She's vaguely familiar, but with her baseball cap and sunglasses I don't know who she is. I stay behind Cole in case it's one of my mother's friends. With one final glare she goes on her way and I sigh with relief.

"You okay?" Cole drops my hand as he turns to examine me. I miss his touch already. "Oh boy, you're bleeding!"

I glance down at my leg to see that he's right. Now I know what the sharp thing was. Or what it did, anyway. "It's just a scratch."

But he's crouched down in front of me examining my leg. "Come on, we'll go down to the water to wash the blood off."

"What about the sharks?" I giggle. Blood in the water can attract sharks, sure, but I'm not going to be swimming with them.

Cole rolls his eyes, but I see a hint of a grin. He stands and grabs my hand again, pulling me behind him.

We stop at the sand dunes to take off our shoes. Cole whips his shirt over his head before grabbing our shoes and bags and reclaiming my hand. *Oh boy.* Boys got abs. The full six pack, who knew.

He tugs on my hand and we head onto the sand, straight for the water. He drops our things above the high tide line without stopping. When we get to the water he lets go of my hand and continues into the surf, leaving me on the edge. Wish I had my swimmers. He dives into the waves, still holding his shirt, and pops up on the other side of the breakers. Then he turns and body surfs back to where I'm standing. Guess he doesn't have his surfboard with him today, not that he needs it.

He rises from the water, an Adonis, water streaming down his lean, tan body. He shakes the water out of his hair and I shriek and jump back as it splashes me. It's cold, despite the hot day.

Actually the day isn't all that's hot although I don't want to admit it. His hair has gone super curly from the salt water and I want to touch his abs. I lift my eyes to find him grinning at me. I look pointedly at the surf, then back at him, an eyebrow raised. Maybe he'll forget that he caught me staring at his stomach.

"Sorry, couldn't resist. The water called me."

I realise he's apologising for going in for a swim, not for splashing me. *That'd be right.*

Then he drops to his knees in front of me and begins wiping the blood from my scratch with his wet shirt. I feel bad for thinking mean thoughts.

I suck in my breath with a hiss. "That stings!"

"Don't be a baby." He continues wiping blood away, rinsing the shirt in the ocean once. "It's not too deep. Just bled a lot. The salt water will do it good."

He sloshes his shirt in the water one last time before standing in a fast, graceful movement, and wringing the water out of the shirt. He slings it over one shoulder.

"You going in?"

I shake my head. "Two reasons. One, I'm bleeding. I've got no desire to be shark bait. And two, no swimmers. I can't exactly go into the water in my underwear."

He waggles his eyebrows suggestively. "You could. I think you'd rock that look."

I huff and he holds up both hands. "Just saying."

"I'm not a boy. Girls don't do things like that."

"I'll warn you next time, so you can come prepared."

"Next time?" I arch a brow at him.

"You're officially a wagger now."

"And you're officially a bad influence."

But I needed this. I take a deep breath of the fresh salty air. For the first time all day I feel free.

10 GROUNDED

The feeling of freedom stays with me Friday night and lasts until Saturday afternoon.

I spent Friday night doing makeup videos to put up on my Instagram. I tagged Hannah when I posted the first one so she'll be able to learn how to do the 'natural look' concealer and base.

My phone was propped up beside my mirror and I forgot it was there. I pretended I was talking to Hannah, showing her all the tricks, and went from base to contouring to brows, eyes and lips, all natural. Then I added a layer to glam it up. Including the eyelash flick. I had so many video's I was embarrassed to post them all at once. So I figured out how to schedule them to post once a week until they're all uploaded. #Perfect.

It felt good to be doing something to help other people and made me forget about my hot mess audition for a while.

Now we're on our way from pony club to baseball, Mum driving.

"Is there something you want to tell me?"

I immediately feel guilty. Mum's using the voice. The

you've let me down voice, which makes you feel guilty and ready to beg forgiveness whether you've done something wrong or not. And I haven't done anything wrong. Nothing Mum knows about, anyway.

"About yesterday," prompts Mum.

Oh boy. A cold feeling settles over me. There's no way she could know about the audition.

Is there?

"Because Mrs Stewart saw you at the beach with a boy. "

I feel a rush of relief. She knows that I ditched school. I should've recognised the woman with the dog yesterday. Her daughter, Sarah, does pony club with Jenna. She would have made sure to catch up with Mum this morning, no doubt.

"Who was the boy? And why weren't you at school?"

"You're in trouble," my little sister singsongs under her breath.

"You don't know him. And it was spur of the moment. A one-time thing. I've never done anything like that before, I swear." It comes out in a rush, the words tumbling over each other. I'm so grateful she doesn't know about the audition that I don't realize how much trouble I'm in until it's too late.

"Victoria." Mum's voice is ice. "I won't have you ruining your reputation by running around with wild boys. And leaving school? I can't believe you did that. What's gotten into you?"

"I didn't—"

She keeps talking over me. "You're grounded. If you're not at one of your pre-planned activities or at school, then you're at home. And you will stay at school, young lady. Even if I have to put a tracking device on your ankle. "

"There's an app for that on your phone," says Jenna helpfully.

I glare at her.

"What have you got to say for yourself?"

"I'm sorry." My voice is small. "It was a mistake."

Mum looks grim. Her hands are clenched on the steering wheel, knuckles white. "Who were you with?"

"Um..." Cole is exactly the sort of wild boy Mum doesn't want me hanging around with. He surfs, he parties, and he has a motorbike. Lucky guy, having his licence already. That sort of freedom would be nice. He lived with his mum in the caravan park, until they moved in next door. But I can't tell her any of that. "I don't know."

Mum's grip on the wheel gets even tighter. "Tori," she says through gritted teeth.

But what can she do. I'm already grounded. "How long am I grounded for?" I make an effort to change the subject.

"For the rest of your life."

"Mum!" I know she's not serious.

"Two weeks, Tori."

"Whatever." In reality, it's not that big a deal, not that I'd tell Mum that. I suspect my party invites are going to be nonexistent with Veronica in the picture. I'd be staying at home anyway. Being grounded is actually a good thing. It gives me an excuse.

I groan and rub my hands over my face. What has my life become so that being grounded is a good thing?

I'm so messed up.

But at least I didn't drag Cole into it with me.

11 CASTING CALL

It's been a long weekend, waiting until Monday rolls around to find out if I got Beauty. I should have put down a backup role. Stupid.

No, Tori. Have a bit of faith in yourself.

When I get to school I go straight to the drama room, where the list is pinned on the notice board in the back of the room. Miss will go through it with us today in class, but everyone wants to know straight away.

There's already a crowd gathered around, and silence falls as I walk into the room and kids notice me. The whispers start. Usually it wouldn't bother me, it would be about my new hairstyle or something. But I see pity in some eyes, and gloating in some of the others. My bad feeling is back, the butterflies doing their dance in my belly.

"How bad is it," says a voice in my ear. I don't turn around.

"Don't know yet, I just got here."

An arm is slung over my shoulders and Cole pulls me along with him as he pushes through to the noticeboard. The other kids make way for him. The looks have changed.

The girls are checking him out and the guys are standing taller. One of them fist bumps him. It's always been this way with Cole.

He ignores them all except the fist-bump guy. He's always done that too. It's like he doesn't even notice. Maybe he doesn't.

On Friday I had almost convinced myself that I'd over-reacted. My audition wasn't that awful, and even if it wasn't my best work, my version of Beauty was so much closer to the script than Veronica's that they'd have to give the part to me regardless. Now I'm not so sure.

We finally get to the list and I almost can't look. The parts are listed on the left and the person who got the role on the right, with the understudy in brackets beside them. Other lists are pinned to the board for the backstage crews. Costumes. Lighting. Stagehand. Props, and so on.

I take a deep breath and scan down the cast list quickly.

Beast— Scotty. No surprise there. The understudy is some kid, Josh, who I don't know very well.

Beauty— Veronica.

Gut punch. I'd been expecting the worst but to see it there in black and white is devastating. I can't be the under-study to Veronica, I just can't.

Then I realise I won't have to. The name written neatly in brackets beside Veronica's isn't mine. It's Talia's. She's a year ten student and I've heard reports she's good. But Miss said she'd give preference to the year elevens this year. My eyes prickle and my throat gets tight. I won't cry in front of everyone, I won't.

I glance at Cole. He's not looking at the cast list. I don't know if he looked at it at all, I was too focused. He's studying the other lists, for the backup crews.

He shoulder-bumps me.

"Looks like you got your first choice," he says, loud enough for those close by to hear but not shouting. I glance up at him and he winks. Then he points to one of the lists. I squint. I'm so surprised at his comments that my tears have vanished but I'm still having trouble focusing.

He's pointing to the makeup list. "I still remember that zombie you did for Halloween in Year eight. It was insane."

Sure enough, my name is third from the bottom for the makeup crew. I vaguely remember putting it as one of my choices on Friday, my encounter with Hannah still fresh in my mind. One of the other names on the list catches my eye and I groan inwardly. Cassie. And Sam too. Oh joy, guess I'm going to get to prove that I'm over Jack.

Remembering our audience, I shrug. "Yeah, first choice. Yay me. What did you get?"

He points to another list. "Lighting."

"Cool. Okay, I've got to go." I shrug his arm off my shoulder and pivot. Standing right behind me is Veronica and flanking her are Josephine and Tiffany. Veronica doesn't say a word but her face says it all. Superior, smug even.

"I guess they liked my interpretation better than yours," she says.

I force a smile into my voice. "Yep. Have fun learning all those lines."

"I already know them. My old school did *Beauty and the Beast* last term, remember? This will be a piece of cake."

It must have been a big deal, she's only told everyone a million times.

What do you say to that?

My mind is blank but Cole comes to my rescue.

"Hope you don't get bored, then, doing the same old,

same old." He gives her a cool onceover then turns to me. "Coming?"

He saunters away. I'm not sure why he's helping. Again. But I'll take it.

"Later," I say breezily to Veronica and the other girls. Veronica rolls her eyes, but Tiffany and Jo look gob smacked. They clearly already knew Veronica was in and I was out. They also knew how badly I wanted it. Not even that. I expected it. There wasn't a doubt in my mind about this part until Fridays audition, and I hadn't made a secret of it. So they would have been expecting a scene. A melt down even. I'm not going to give them the satisfaction.

Now I've just got to survive the rest of the day.

If only it were that simple.

In a lot of ways, it is simple. It's just not easy.

Everybody seems to be talking about me. I know this because of the furtive looks and whispers, and the way conversations stop, or become loud and over the top ordinary, whenever I walk past.

'Isn't it hot today?' Nobody ever talks about the weather. 'Did you hear they've got a new flavoured milk at the canteen?' Nobody ever talks about canteen food either.

I sigh as I round the corner and yet another group of year ten kids nudge each other and look knowingly at me, then each other. I ignore them and beeline for my classroom. It's maths and I'm the first one there so I sit in my usual seat in the back row. I wait to see if Tiffany sits beside me. She doesn't. She walks in, deep in conversation with another girl and they go right past without even saying hi. I'd think they didn't see me, but I heard some of their conversation and they were talking about something that was on the news this morning. As if Tiffany watches the news.

By the time we get to the afternoon assembly I've had enough.

When one of the younger girls, a year seven newbie, approaches, I want to ignore her but she reminds me too much of my little sister.

"Excuse me, I just want to thank you," she says. Her face is red and she won't meet my eye. I'm not sure why she's thanking me and my brow furrows.

"For the video." She shuffles her feet and peeks up from under her fringe. "I don't have a mum or sister to teach me how to do my make up, so, yeah. Thank you."

"Oh." This isn't about the play at all. I smile at her. "You're welcome. I've got some more coming out, every Friday."

"Cool." She smiles, shuffles her feet, then turns to go back to her friends. "See-ya Tori," she throws over her shoulder. "I can't wait until Friday!"

Smiling to myself, I walk into the hall and find a seat. I don't even care that I'm sitting on my own.

There's all the usual 'school spirit' stuff and then we collect our report cards. I'm under strict instructions from my parents not to open it until I get home, where they, in fact, will open, dissect, and then discuss.

Fun times.

I don't want to go home, but the final bell signals the end of the assembly and the school day.

I've made it through the day— barely— and can escape. I clutch the yellow envelope containing my report card firmly in my hand. I've always been good at school, what with the tutoring and strictly enforced study sessions. I'm pretty confident in my results. The day can only improve from here.

12 ESCAPE

One thing I'm starting to realise is that you should never tell yourself things can't get any worse. Optimism is overrated. It's pretty depressing as I've always considered myself a positive person. But no amount of positive vibes are going to change the Bs on my report card into As.

I mean, it's not all Bs. There's only two subjects I'm not doing well. Maths, which we already knew, hence the tutoring. And I think I've done well to get my mark up to a B if we're being honest. I was a steady C before tutoring and I've worked hard. I'm kind of proud of myself. But it's not good enough for my mother.

It's all relative for her. Relative to what she thinks I should have got, I've failed. If she's going to fork out good money on tutoring, then she expects better. And even though PE, my other B, isn't important in the big picture the fact that I only got a B means that I didn't try hard enough. It was nothing to do with the fact that I hate ball sports, which has been the focus the last two terms.

"It's a good thing you're already grounded," she says.

"But it's not enough. You're losing phone privileges until you can prove to me that you're really trying."

"Mum!" I can't believe this. "I *am* trying. You don't know how hard I've been working. I'm doing my best. It's not my fault—"

"Enough!" It's like a whip crack across my face. She doesn't touch me physically, she never would. But she can silence me in a second. There's no talking back, no defending yourself, and no way of winning. Not when she's in this mood.

If only Dad had been home when she opened the report card it wouldn't have been so bad. He softens her, somehow. Maybe he'll talk to her when he gets home from work.

"Hand it over." Her hand is outstretched, her foot tapping impatiently.

Reluctantly, I go to my bag and pull out my phone. I hold in the power button to turn it off. I don't want her seeing all my notifications. That would be too much. It's password protected so she can't get into it without me knowing. Surely, she wouldn't go that far.

But taking the phone off me seems to be enough for now.

"We've already talked about your grounding, but just to reiterate," she says, my phone held securely in her hand. "No extracurricular activities unless I've given my approval. Tutoring, swimming, pony club and the rehearsals for your school play once they begin. That's it. No youth group."

"But Mum—" Maybe she'll listen to reason.

"No, Victoria. You obviously don't have enough time to study and you've got enough going on as it is without youth group. You're grounded for four weeks and that's the end of it."

"Four weeks?" I can't believe it. "But last week you said two weeks."

"That was last week. And now it's four weeks. Do you want to argue back anymore?"

"Fine. Can I go now?" I'm annoyed about youth group because it's one of the few things I do that's actually fun. But I'm relieved she hasn't found out that I missed out on the role of Beauty.

Maybe I should tell her. Get it all over with at once? But I don't think I can handle any more criticism right now. Or any more weeks being added onto my time. Jeez, at this rate I'll be stuck at home, with no phone, until I finish school.

"You've got an hour until dinner," she says. "Think about how you can improve your marks."

She turns and goes into the kitchen still holding my phone. I see her drop it into the junk drawer. Good to know, but it won't help. I'm not getting that baby back until Mum feels like giving it to me. I'm just lucky she didn't take my iPad and computer as well.

I go up to my room and retrieve my sketchbook from the locked drawer. I take it and my pencil case with me and sneak back downstairs. Not sneaking, I correct myself. Being quiet. I slip through the laundry and out the back door without being seen. There's some sort of commotion happening next door. Yelling and such. It was loud over there when I got home from school, so it's been going on for a while. Maybe they're cheering a football game or some-thing. Not my problem, though. I've got enough of my own.

I make my way to the old fig tree. There's a ladder at the back, out of sight of the house, and nestled up in the branches is my escape. My treehouse. I've cleaned it up and brought a yoga mat and cushions to sit on. There's a plastic tub with a secure lid to keep them in, spider free and water proof, for when I'm not using them. I also keep an emergency stash of muesli bars and a six-pack of water that I replenish when it gets low. My chocolate supply is limited but occasionally I'll smuggle some up here to eat guilt free. Last week I managed to snag a whole family block of Cadbury's peppermint chocolate, my favourite. Mum picked it up by accident in the supermarket and no-one else in the family will touch it, so it's mine. I'm looking forward to it, I need a chocolate fix right about now. My treehouse is my refuge, my happy spot, where I can get away from everyone.

I climb the ladder and poke my head up through the gap in the floorboards which acts as the doorway. I fling my sketchbook and pencils onto the old boards and they slide along the floor. The sun is low in the sky, blinding me momentarily as I climb after them. There's a a soft thud, as my sketchbook connects with something solid. The wall should be further away, the sound came too early for the amount of force I put into the throw. It's followed almost immediately by another noise. An 'oof', like the air being knocked out of someone. I recoil, stifling a scream as I try not to panic.

There's someone here. Someone in my treehouse.

I scramble backwards as I try to focus on the shape on the floor. I miscalculate the distance to the hole that's the only way out of here and next thing I know I'm falling. My foot scrapes along the ladder, fast, and my arms are flailing. My life flashes before my eyes as things seem to slow down. I won't get to kiss Cole before I die, I think; regret a bitter taste in my mouth. *Where did that thought come from?*

A hand closes around my wrist and time snaps back into place. I'm being hauled back up the ladder, none too gently, and end up on the floor of the tree house glaring at my saviour. He blocks the sun, so I can see who it is for the first time. He's got a halo effect going on, making him look like an angel. He's no angel. Although he's been coming to my rescue quite a bit lately. But that doesn't give him a free pass to my happy place.

"Cole? What the hell are you doing in my treehouse?"

13 GOOD EXPLANATION

Cole smirks, and releases my hand. "Your happy place?"

I groan, burying my face in my hands. "Treehouse. I said treehouse."

"Sure you did."

I drop my hands and look around. He's got my yoga mat unrolled, cushions piled on top. There's a bottle of water, half empty, on the floor. And that's not all.

"Did you eat my chocolate?" The wrapper is crumpled on the floor beside the water bottle, evidence of his crime.

"I was hungry." There's a tiny smudge of chocolate at the corner of his mouth. It should look disgusting but suddenly I want to kiss him, to see if he tastes like peppermint chocolate. Disgusted with myself I go on the attack.

"You don't eat a block of chocolate if you're hungry. There's muesli bars right there."

I look in the box and that's when I see the empty muesli bar wrappers.

"You ate my muesli bars too?" My voice is high pitched and shrieky.

Cole's shoulders are shaking and I realise he's trying not to laugh. I can't believe this boy. The silent laughing stops as he takes in my glare.

"I'll buy you some more. And chocolate too," he says. "I'm sorry, okay? I'm stranded at home and there's no food in the house."

"You're having muesli bars and chocolate for dinner?" I wish my family was the sort who would welcome strays, and I could bring him up to the house with me for dinner. But I can't. My family isn't that sort of family, and even if they were, I'm grounded and this is Cole Black. All hell would break loose if Mum knew he was here.

My mind flicks back to the noise I heard next door, earlier.

"Does your Mum watch football?" I ask.

"What? No. And it's none of your business what I have for dinner." He seems to realise he's being aggressive and shuffles back to lean against the wall. He'd been on his knees in an awkward crouch. Nobody can stand up in this treehouse, not unless they're five.

"Sorry!" I shuffle myself back to the other side and lean against that wall, mirroring his position. We're in a standoff. So much for the kiss. Now I just want him to leave.

"So." We both speak at the same time. Our eyes connect and there's pain in his. They're red-rimmed and it looks like he's been crying.

Surely not? This is Cole Black.

"Are you alright?" I ask softly. His parents, or rather, his mum and the greasy guy, must be fighting if they weren't cheering on a football game. I can't imagine that. My parents argue sometimes, but they never yell or throw things.

He rubs his face with his hands, breaking the stare. He

nods into his hands, and then looks back up at me. "Yeah, why wouldn't I be?"

I frown, but let it go. Let him have his pretences. Then I notice the sleeping bag spread out on top of the yoga mat.

"Are you planning on sleeping up here?" I point to the sleeping bag. I hadn't noticed it before because of the glare.

There's a loud crashing sound from next door and more yelling. Cole flinches, and his hands curl into fists.

"Is that alright with you? I don't want to be at home at the moment." He's looking at me intently.

I hold his gaze and nod.

"I'd take you home with me for dinner, but my Mum's in a bad mood too." There's another crash. "Nothing like that, though."

"It's her dropkick boyfriend. They do nothing but fight and if I'm there I want to get in the middle of it, which makes things worse."

"He hits her?" I widen my eyes. "Or you?"

Cole shakes his head. "No, that hasn't happened. Just the yelling and throwing things. I thought the money would make things better, but it hasn't."

He rolls his shoulders and shakes his hands out. This boy has been nothing but good to me this week. What's been going on with me, with Veronica and the play, is nothing compared to what he's got going on at home. But he's helped me no end. Giving up my treehouse and some muesli bars for a night is the least I can do.

"You can't let my mum know you're here," I say suddenly. "She doesn't like you." I realise how that sounds. "She doesn't like anyone."

"It's okay, she's never liked me." The corner of his mouth rises. "Not many mothers do. I know what they say. We're poor and my Dad ran off. And I ride a motorbike.

Everyone looks down on us and having money doesn't change that."

"You're right. But having money, or not, doesn't change who you are. And you're just as good as anyone else. Better than the ones who say stuff like that, that's for sure." I meet his eyes without blinking. I'm not sure what made me blurt all that but it's true. He's the first to look away. His glance flicks to the sketchbook on the floor beside him. I hope he doesn't pick it up but I'm too scared to make any sudden moves towards it in case he realises how important it is to me. I'm watching him, watching my sketchbook, so when he looks back he catches me staring. My face heats, but fortunately it's dark so he can't see.

I hope. He's scrutinising me closely. Jeez, maybe he can see me blush.

His hand snakes out towards my sketchbook but he doesn't break eye contact. I see the movement in my peripheral vision.

Oh no. He's not.

I lunge for the sketchbook, launching myself across the small space and sliding over the floor. My fingertips touch the cover just as it's snatched from my grasp. Momentum keeps me moving until my head collides with Cole's stomach. He lets an 'ooof', the same sound I heard when I climbed up the ladder.

I'm disoriented and it takes me a moment to work out how his stomach came to be where my head is. I'd knocked the sketchbook away from his hand with my lunge, I realise, and he had to stretch full length to get to it before me.

I groan. Cole has my sketchbook. He's up on one elbow, dangling it over my head with his other hand.

"Looking for something?" His grin is teasing but the glint in his eye is wicked. Our heads are close enough to touch. To kiss. All he'd have to do is lean down, or I could reach up and pull him closer. The moment stretches between us and neither of us blinks. The sketchbook is forgotten. He licks his lips and my tongue mimics the action. His head moves a fraction closer and my breath catches in my chest. I really want him to kiss me, and I think he's going to.

His mouth inches closer and I have a choice to make. The kiss or my sketchbook.

I might regret this if it's the only chance I get to kiss Cole Black, but in this moment, I choose my privacy. I grab for my sketchbook, snatching it out of Cole's hand and rolling away. I'm almost graceful as I flip over and scoot back to my original position against the far wall. *Yeah, right.*

Cole blinks, then sits up and leans against the wall opposite me. We're mirror images.

When he speaks his tone is carefully casual, changing the subject but also telling me that he really wants to know my answer.

"So, what are you doing here?" he asks.

I consider lying for a nanosecond, then it all comes pouring out.

"I'm in trouble with Mum. She grounded me on Saturday, and then tonight I lost my *phone privileges.*"

"Why? What happened? I thought you were a *good girl.*"

"It's your fault I got grounded," I say. "That lady we almost ran over at the beach told Mum she saw me. Turns out her daughter goes to pony club."

I scoff. "I thought she looked familiar."

"Sorry." He looks contrite for a moment before he frowns. "Did you tell her it was my fault?"

"Of course not!" My glare could melt glaciers. "I'm not a dobber."

"You might have got off a bit lighter if you'd told. I wouldn't blame you." He shrugs. "I've got broad shoulders, I can handle the haters."

I shake my head. "I wouldn't do that. I chose to go with you. That's on me, not you."

"Well, thanks." He leans his head back against the wall and closes his eyes. "So why did you lose your phone? Did you kill someone?"

"No." I sigh. "I got two Bs on my report card."

"That's harsh." His eyes open but his head doesn't move. "My mum doesn't care about that sort of thing. I sometimes think it would be nice if she did."

"You don't want the punishment, believe me. It's four weeks. And I've got to *prove myself* and earn back my privileges."

I mimic his pose, leaning my head back against the wall and closing my eyes for a moment. "I'm just glad she doesn't know that I missed out on the lead in the play."

"Seriously?"

"Yep. Deadly serious. It's a big deal to her, and I don't know what she'll do when she finds out." I shudder. "I probably won't ever be allowed to leave the house again except for school. She might even decide to home-school me."

Cole whistles. "That bad, huh. You know, it seems to me that she just wants the best for you."

I snort. "She has a funny way of showing it."

"What are you going to do? Why don't you talk to her about it?"

I shake my head. "She wouldn't listen. No, I've got to figure out a way to win back Beauty before she finds out."

14 SABOTAGE

Coles' head comes forward, away from the wall, and he's looking at me intently. "What's the plan?"

"I haven't thought it through very far. But first I have to talk to Miss Pretty and get her to make me an understudy for Beauty. There's a precedent for having two for the main role. They did it last year with *Peter Pan*." I sigh. "If I can't do that, I might as well just confess to Mum and be done with it."

"Assuming that works, what next? You'll still have to get rid of two people before you get the lead role."

"I know. That's the hard part."

"Want some help? I like a challenge."

My eyebrows rise. "You'd help?"

"Of course." He smirks. "Sabotage is my specialty."

It's a great line but I don't believe him. "Seriously?" My lip curls and I wrinkle my nose.

Cole looks uncomfortable. "There was that one time at band camp—"

"I think that was a movie."

He holds up his hands. "Okay, okay. I was just trying to help, you're going to need it. And I've got some ideas. But if you don't want my help—"

I'm still dubious but he's right. I do need help. I sigh. "Okay, hotshot. Bring it on. But answer one question first. And I want you to be serious."

He frowns, but nods. "What is it?"

"For real this time. Why are you being so nice to me this past week?"

I can't really tell in this light, but he seems to go red. He ducks his head, so I can't see his face. Is he embarrassed?

"Well?"

"It's just—" He stops and takes a deep breath. He holds my gaze and starts talking again. "To start with it was because I didn't want you blabbing to people about me moving in next door to you. Our situation has changed, but I don't want everyone to know about it. I was looking for you that first day at school to talk to you and I heard those girls, your so-called friends, giving you a hard time. I didn't like it." He's frowning now, and I motion with my hand for him to continue.

"I've never liked those girls." He holds eye contact and I find I can't look away. "More to the point, I don't like who you've become since you've been hanging around them."

"Uh, they're hanging around me."

"Yeah, I guess. You've changed since primary school and I get it, it was become one of them or be eaten alive. That was kind of my fault too."

"Yeah, it was." The spelling bee incident the first day of high school was definitely his fault.

"I never meant for you to be made fun of. I was a bit clueless back then. I mean, it was a joke, but I didn't expect the kids to be so nasty about it."

"It surprised me too. And not in a good way." The kids were so mean I went home in tears every day for a week. He'd told the office ladies that I won the year six spelling bee competition at state level, the week before school went back. I don't even know how he knew about it. Of course, the office ladies told the principal who announced it at assembly to congratulate me. I could have died.

It was a big deal in primary school which is why I'd been pushed into it by Mum. And thanks to her *encouragement and support,* I'd won. And hoped it would never be mentioned again.

Let me just say, spelling bees are not cool in high school. I mean, I already knew that. But it was rammed home that day and the week that followed by all the kids who came up and asked me to spell ridiculous words, like ectoplasm, and then sniggered behind their cupped hands to their friends. Or to my face.

The first time it happened I actually started spelling the word out loud before I realised they were having a go at me. I wised up pretty fast and I've held a grudge against Cole Black ever since.

Nope, we're not friends nowadays.

Although we're acting more like besties at the moment. It's nice having someone to talk to about this stuff, actually. Tiffany and Jo might be my best friends, but we never talk. Not real talk. When I think about it, we're not close that way. Sure, I know the names of their brothers and sisters, and when their birthdays are. But secret hopes and dreams? Boy crush—the real one—not the one they say because it's the popular choice? Favourite thing to do outside of school? I don't know any of that. We simply don't talk about that stuff.

Are we really friends at all? I tuck that thought away to

think about later and turn my attention back to Cole. For some reason I want to explain myself.

"I made a decision back then— never to be in that position again. Everyone was going to like me. I wanted to be the popular one."

"I'm sorry about that." He sounds sincere.

I wave it away. "It is what it is. But this week, it's been just like back in year seven again." I swallow hard. "I can't believe it can be taken away from me so easily. I've worked really hard to be the popular one. And it is work, believe me. Mum wanting me to be perfect at everything doesn't help. But I made it, I was home free, and only one year to go before school's done."

"And then the new girl came along."

"Yep." I look at him. "Why is she targeting me, Cole? What did I ever do to her?"

He's silent for a moment before answering slowly. "I don't think it's personal. I think she wants to be at the top of the pecking order and not a bottom feeder. It's hard for new kids, you know how it is."

I nod.

"And the easiest way to get to the top is to take out the current leader. That's you, Tori. The fact that you weren't around these holidays made it even easier for her. She was able to slip in and cement a few key friendships without you even being aware of the threat until it was too late."

"That actually makes a lot of sense. How do you know?"

He shrugs. "It's what I'd do if I had to go to a new school. If I cared about being popular."

I scoff. "You don't have to even try. Everyone thinks you're cool. And you don't even care.

"Or do I?" He waggles his eyebrows. "Maybe that's just what I want everyone to think."

"Nah, you don't care. If you did, you'd be dating the most popular girl. That's me in case you were wondering."

"Not any more, Tori, Tori." He repeats his words from that first day on the bench when he told me I've got to pick my battles. "But— are you asking me out? It might be your only hope of getting your friends back."

"Are you asking *me* out?" I'm so confused and then I can't help myself. I break out in a case of the giggles. They bubble up from inside me as the ridiculousness of this situation hits me. Sitting here in my treehouse with Cole Black discussing popularity and dating. It's hilarious.

Cole looks at me like I'm weird, and then he joins me. Laughing is contagious, after all.

15 ABANDONED

It's become clear by the end of the week that my friends have abandoned me. I haven't been kicked out of the group, but I'm not in charge any more. Not by a long shot.

It's *Vee says this*, and *Vee does that*. And they're not talking about me when they say it. I'm conflicted. On the one hand I'm gutted by the loss, not being the one they all look to. But on the other hand, I'm enjoying the lack of pressure. I hadn't realised how much pressure it was to be the one making all the decisions.

But mostly I'm sad. I turn to tell Jo something and she's not walking with me, she's up ahead with Veronica. Or I'm sitting next to an empty seat and Tiff walks right past me to sit next to Veronica.

I haven't seen Cole, not that I thought he'd hang out with me all day, but after our conversation in the treehouse I expected something more. I thought we'd connected.

I'm just drifting through my days, trying not to show how cut up I am. I've never felt more alone than I do right now.

THURSDAY AFTERNOON I stay back after drama.

"Can I talk to you, Miss Pretty?" I ask.

"Is it about Beauty?" she asks. "Because I want you to know that it was very close with you and Talia."

I swallow and wipe my sweaty hands subtly on my skirt.

"That's what I wanted to talk to you about. It's just, she's only in Year Ten and you said that seniors would get preference."

She sighs. "I know. But I was overruled. If there was a way around it, I'd pick you in a heartbeat."

It hadn't occurred to me that Miss Pretty didn't get the final say. I knew there was a group of teachers involved with the production, but I thought Miss Pretty was in charge. Miss is still talking.

"I know you had your heart set on Beauty, but you over-played it. You were way too theatrical. This is a hard lesson for you, but sometimes you need to let your emotions show. Like we did in class the first day back. You could learn a thing or two from Veronica, actually."

I take a moment to let that sink in. It sucks, but I know she's right. I made the wrong choice for the audition and they should have picked Veronica. But I know I can do better. I was made for this role, Beauty, I just need the chance to prove it.

Oh well, here goes nothing. I take a deep breath then blurt it out.

"Can I be second understudy?"

Miss is shaking her head, so I rush on. "Like we did last year with Romeo and Juliette. We had two understudies for that."

Miss looks dubious. "I don't know, Tori. That was a much bigger production."

"Please, Miss Pretty. Pretty please."

She laughs at my play on words and hope leaps in my chest.

"Okay, but on one condition."

My squeal of joy dies in my chest.

"You'll have to keep doing your back-stage role too. Costumes and makeup, wasn't it? You can learn all the parts for Beauty, but it's unlikely you'll get to play her. It would be very unfortunate if both Veronica and Talia were unable to perform. So I'll need you to keep up with the backstage job you were assigned. Can you do that?"

I'm not happy, but I nod. At least I'm now the third understudy. Or equal second. Yep, I like equal second better. Now to knock out the competition.

Challenge accepted.

OUR FIRST REHEARSAL meeting is the following Monday after school. The previous week went fast, my programmed extracurricular activities kept me busy. I haven't seen much of Cole and the yelling next door has quietened down, so I've been able to reclaim my treehouse. It's my one bit of sanity. I go out there most afternoons with my sketchbook and draw. I draw all sorts of things. My clothing designs are a big part of it, but I also do illustrations for the Zen goddess quotes I've been collecting.

Martha started me on this path, coming up with different sayings at the end of each yoga class over the holidays. Things like, 'What we think, we become - Buddha' and one of her own which was 'I walk my own path in life.

Your approval is not requested or required.' Martha is a badass.

I've even put my own spin on some. 'Be consistent. Rome wasn't built in a day and neither were the perfect abs.' It's probably lame, but so what? I like it.

I write out the quote calligraphy style and then draw whatever it inspires in me. Dragons, fairies, and roses all feature. I love dragons, especially the western ones like Spyro, with proper legs and wings. I've never been a fan of those worm dragons, the Chinese and Japanese style. Give me a dragon that looks nice and solid any day. With kick-ass wings and breathing fire, of course.

Fairies have wings too. Huh, I've got a theme. I draw gargoyles too. Guess I like mythical creatures that can fly. And all the pretties, flowers and such.

I've been leaving a spare pencil case filled with my drawing implements up in the treehouse. My Gran called them that, and I liked the sound of it and have used it ever since. So I'm only bringing my sketchbook back and forth with me from the house. I've restocked my water and snack supplies since Cole decimated them and got a pleasant surprise one night to find a box of Ferraro Rocher chocolates waiting in the snack box with a note from Cole.

One word. *Enjoy*.

No apology for eating the original block of Cadbury from my stash, but I did enjoy them in one huge binge that left me feeling a little sick afterwards. Next time I'll space them out over a few days. Or weeks. Or maybe even share them with the boy himself. If there is a next time. The thought that there might not be a next time depresses me. I enjoyed our chat that first night, despite the fact he tried to steal my sketchbook. It was nice having someone to talk to about Mum and how unfair she's being.

I've found evidence he's been sleeping up there, but he's avoiding the space while I'm using it. Honestly, I'm grateful. I need my Zen time. But at the same time, I kind of miss him. His sleeping bag and a spare flannelette shirt are tucked into a new plastic tub that he must have brought in. It matches mine and stacks easily, so it doesn't take up any extra space. I'm okay with it, and with him staying there if he needs to. I just wish he'd come and visit me.

Conflicted much? I snort, a half laugh. No, it's strictly business. I need help to come up with some ideas to win back Beauty. Maybe something will leap out at me at rehearsal.

I enter the school hall five minutes early and grab a seat in the back. Miss Pretty and a few other teachers are on stage with a whiteboard.

"Come in closer, everyone. We want you to be able to see the board."

I slink down further in my seat. I'm sure I'll be able to figure it out from back here. It's not rocket science, I've been involved with the school play before. I sigh, and my throat gets tight. This was going to be my big year, the year I was the sole female lead, and I've blown it.

"You okay?" A voice at my ear as Cole slips into the seat beside me.

I glance over at him, trying not to let him see how upset I am. I'm fighting not to burst into tears as it sinks in that it's not me up there in the front row in pride of place.

I bend down to dig through my bag for the hankie I've got floating at the bottom ,so I can sneakily wipe my eyes. When I sit back up Cole's watching me.

He nudges my shoulder with his. "Hey, it will all work out. You'll see."

I flash him a weak smile and turn my attention back to

Miss Pretty. A moment later Cole grabs my hand. He laces our fingers together, his palm warm and comforting. I look over in surprise, but he's got his eyes glued to the stage, all nonchalant. He squeezes my hand but doesn't say anything. I'm confused. Maybe he just wants me to know I'm not alone? It's not like anyone can see us back here, so it's not about appearances.

Or maybe he likes me.

I smile.

Maybe I like him too.

16   NEW FRIENDS

fter laying out the rehearsal timetable and what each team in the backstage crew is expected to do, Miss Pretty gets us to break up into our separate groups. That's means Costumes and makeup for me, and lighting for Cole.

"Good luck," he says. "Meet me back here when we're done."

I nod, and then take off down the stairs toward the backstage area as fast as I can. I feel strangely self-conscious. There's people milling around everywhere and it takes me a while to work out that the costumes crew is in the dressing rooms.

I hear voices as I walk towards the open door and as I draw closer they become clearer.

"Have we got the right room? Where is everybody?" A girl's voice. She sounds familiar, but I can't place her.

"They'll get here. Patience, grasshopper." Another girl. Also familiar but I can't place her either. "Say, what do you think about Cole and the biatch? They've been pretty friendly lately."

"I don't care, as long as she stays away from Jack."

I stop when I realise who it is. That's Cassie Parish, and the other person must be Samantha Hill. My face heats as I realise they're talking about what happened last term when I was trying to get Jack Jones to ask me out. It was too little, too late. He was already hooked on Cassie when I made my play. I never stood a chance.

"She never stood a chance. He could see through her a mile off. Phonies aren't his thing," says Sam.

My blood boils and before I can stop myself I'm through the door and in her face. "I'm not a phoney. Take that back."

Sam is startled and takes a step back, holding her hands up in the 'stop' position. Then her expression hardens. "Victoria. If you can't handle the truth you shouldn't slink around eavesdropping."

"And you shouldn't talk about people behind their back."

"Oh, I'm happy to say it to your face. You were a real biatch to Cassie last term. It was obvious she and Jack had a thing, and you just stomped right in and tried to steal him anyway."

"I did not! Anyone who knows me knows I wouldn't do a thing like that. I thought I had a shot with him and I took it. I knew it was a long shot, but it was a 'now or never' kind of thing." I look between Sam and Cassie and direct my final words to Cassie. I feel bad, in hindsight, for trying to win Jack over. But my mother was hassling me to go out with Trent Riordan and I thought that if I could find someone by myself I could get her to leave me alone.

Not that I'm telling them that.

I hold Cassie's gaze steadily. "When he said no I backed off."

Cassie nods, slowly. "The thing is, we don't know you.

You've never even said hello to me. We've definitely never had a conversation."

It's true, I realise. I don't think anyone really knows me. Hiding in plain sight. It's safe, but it's lonely.

Before I can reply someone walks in. I've got my back to the door, so I don't see who it is, but the looks on Cassie's and Sam's faces are enough for me to know it's a teacher. They practically come to attention.

"Hello, Miss," says Cassie. "Is this the right room for costumes and makeup?"

There's several new teachers this term and I haven't met them all yet. It's not like I care, I won't have anything to do with them unless they're teaching one of the classes I'm in.

"You're in the right place. There should be a few more people on our team. Tori, can you see if you can round them up?"

I know the voice, but I can't put a face to it. I'm having a bad day when it comes to voice recognition. It must be one of my teachers seeing as she knows my name. Most of the teachers call me Victoria, so it's a bit odd that she's used Tori. Word must have got around about my new preference.

I turn around to face the door and freeze. Then all my breath leaves me in a delighted squeal. "Martha! What are you doing here?"

Martha is smiling warmly at me and I leap forward to hug her. She shakes her head subtly. Hugging is a no-no between teachers and students, and that's what she is. She's my new teacher. I quickly morph my attempted hug into a handshake, holding my hand out for her to shake. She clasps my hand, resting her other palm lightly on my forearm. "Tori, it's *so* good to see you."

She's my favourite person in the world, not only my holiday yoga teacher, but a fellow artist. She's a teacher up in Bonalbo, my Gram's home town. Or at least, she was two weeks ago when I saw her last. "Are you teaching here now?"

She nods. "Sorry I didn't tell you about my transfer. It was only finalised this week. Surprise! I'm your new art teacher."

"This is so fantastic!" I'm grinning so wide my mouth almost hurts. "Does this mean I have to call you Miss Mathews?"

Martha laughs. "Nobody is calling me Miss Mathews. Martha, or just Miss if they need to be formal."

A thought occurs to me. "Are you going to run your yoga classes now you're here?" It would be so fantastic to get a dose of Zen goddess yoga goodness every week.

"I am. Just give me a few weeks to settle in."

"You have to come to yoga, you guys." I turn to Cassie and Sam who are looking gob smacked. Whether it's at my enthusiasm or Martha's stunning looks, I'm not sure.

Something I haven't mentioned about Martha yet. She's gorgeous. Her hair is long, black and silky and she's got several thin strands plaited through with bright colours that swirl around and peek out at odd moments. She's tall, almost six foot, and has the lean, lithe build you'd expect from a yoga teacher. Her dress style is a little out there, trending towards flowy skirts like she's wearing today. Usually she pairs them with sandals and a singlet top. Today she's wearing the sandals, but her top is more conservative; it has sleeves and a higher neck than she usually wears. The colours, however, are vibrant. The skirt is multi-coloured and her top is a deep forest green silk which matches one of the swirls in the skirt perfectly, like the jewel in the crown.

Yep. I want to be Martha when I grow up.

"Cassie, Sam, meet Martha. She's the most awesome person I know." The girls move forward and stand there awkwardly.

"Hi Miss, nice to meet you," says Cassie.

"Hi, Miss," mumbles Sam. It's odd to see her without words.

"Hi girls. It's lovely to meet some of Tori's friends. You can call me Martha, or Miss."

They exchange looks at being called my friends but thank goodness they don't say anything.

"Let's see what we've got to work with costume wise. This is going to be so much fun!" Martha claps her hands and marches to the huge cupboards at the back of the room leaving us alone for a moment.

Cassie smiles at me. "You know what, Tori? I think I'm starting to get to know you better already. And so far, so good."

I smile back, my heart feeling lighter for some reason. "Let's start over, can we?" I include both girls in my smile. It's time for a fresh start and maybe even some new friends. "Sam was right. I was a biatch. You were right too, Cassie, we don't know each other. But I'd like to."

"I'd like that too," says Cassie.

Sam rolls her eyes. "Whatever." But she's smiling as she leaves the room to find the others.

17 CATCHUP

There's around a dozen of us in the costume and makeup crew and Martha gets hold of a whiteboard to start mapping out the characters and their costumes for each scene.

The Beast is going to be a lot of fun to create. We're going to make a monster suit for Scotty. He'll wear his basic blacks with padding over the top to make him look bigger. A ginormous set of overalls will go over the top of that and we'll cover them in fake fur. The goal is to keep them easy to remove as he'll have to be in Prince mode as well, and often it's two scenes back to back with different costumes.

We're going to do a full-face cast to make the monster mask. Martha said she'll make it a class project so we'll all get to learn mask-making techniques. Scotty doesn't do art, so those of us in the costume crew will do his face so that, fingers crossed, at least one of the masks will turn out to be usable for the play.

Beauty will need several different costumes. Her basic 'day to day' outfits for when she starts out at home, then once she gets to the castle there will be all the beautiful dresses for her to choose from.

Oh, how I wish it was me.

We won't have to make all Beauty's costumes. We've got a small budget to go vintage dress shopping, there are costumes already in the cupboard from previous productions, and then, for the final big scene, there will be a custom-made dress.

I think of the design in my sketchbook. It would be perfect, even better for the final scene than for scene nine, the one I originally thought to use it for. There's no way I'm going to make it for Veronica though.

Potential sabotage ideas run through my head. I could take in the costumes after she tries them on to make her think she's putting on weight. That would work. Then, of course, the costumes would fit me, and I'd get the role by default.

I frown. That's pretty lame. For starters, Talia is super slim, so she'd just step right in if that were to happen. But what else can I do? Hopefully Cole will have some ideas.

I CATCH up with Cole after we've finished.

"Hey, how was it?" he asks.

"Yeah, good." I smile, surprised that I enjoyed myself. "Cassie and Sam are in my group."

His eyebrows arch. "Is that going to be a problem?"

I shake my head. "Nah, it's all good. We cleared the air and are starting over. At least, I hope so. How was your group?"

"The lighting guys? We're going to have a lot of fun with it. There's some wicked effects we get to play with."

"Really?" I nod, distracted momentarily by the sight of Veronica with Tiffany and Jo up ahead. Before they can see us, I grab Cole's arm and pull him through an open doorway into an empty classroom. "Quick, in here."

Cole glances around the room then sticks his head back out the door.

"Cole!" I whisper-shout.

He looks amused as he turns to face me. "They've gone," he says. "Or did you drag me in here to make out?"

"Yeah, right."

Nervous energy fills me, and I begin to pace. Across to the open windows and back again. I turn to go back to the windows and Cole follows me. As I spin again to keep on pacing he stops me with a hand on my arm. He's standing so close I can feel his body heat hitting me and can see that he has flecks of gold in his green eyes. His eyes blink shut and when he reopens them he clears his throat and takes a step away.

Come back. I miss his closeness already.

I try to speak but have to clear my throat as well.

Then we both start to talk at the same time.

"Jinx!" Again, at the same time. We stand there grinning stupidly at each other for a moment before I wave a hand. "You go."

"No." He waves right back at me. "You first."

I give in, we could be here all day. "I was just going ask if you've come up with any ideas for our plan. Everything I think of is lame."

There's a wicked glint in his eye as he nods. "I've got a few ideas."

"Are you going to tell me?" I want to stamp my foot with impatience. He must notice because his grin grows bigger, wickeder, and gorgeouser.

I mock punch his arm, but it's just an excuse to touch him. I don't know what's come over me. "Tell me already!"

He doesn't answer, simply grabs my hand and pulls me closer to the window.

"Look out, tell me what you see."

I shake my head in frustration. "The oval, trees, the car park."

Now he's shaking his head. "No, not nature and stuff, people. What people do you see?"

"Well." I take a deep breath and concentrate. "There's not many people. Just a few from rehearsals going home."

"Exactly."

"I'm confused. What's your big idea?"

"I'm still working on specifics, but the good part is that now is the perfect time of day to do some behind the scenes sabotage. There's no-one around to catch us."

"So, you don't have any ideas." That's all I take away from his statement.

"I'll come up with something. We can steal her script for starters. If she doesn't have her script, she can't learn her lines."

"She already knows the lines, from when she did the play last time," I say.

"But we're not using the exact same script, are we?" He frowns. "Okay, what else."

"We need to focus on the end goal, which is to get her booted off the play. How do we do that?"

"Maybe we're approaching it all wrong," Cole says. "Maybe instead of getting her booted we need to make her want to quit."

"Genius." My voice contains the utmost sarcasm. "And how do we do that, exactly?"

"Why is she doing this? Is it because it's something she loves? Or is it to stop you from doing it?"

I shake my head. "I don't know, Cole. She put her hand up in the drama class the first week back, then before I knew it she blew me out of the water in the audition and landed the role."

"So it's all about you, then." He nods. "I thought so."

He turns suddenly to fix me with his brilliant stare. "Why does she have it in for you, Tori? What have you done to her?"

"What?" I take a step backwards, away from him, and slam into a desk. I nearly end up on the floor but Cole steps in and saves me, his arms tight around my back. We're chest to chest and my heart is pounding.

What is this boy doing to me?

He lowers his head and for a moment— a moment that seems to lengthen and stretch— I think he's going to kiss me. Then his lips move past my mouth to brush against my ear.

"Easy," he says.

What is it with me, thinking about this boy kissing me?

His warm breath hits my earlobe, sending sparks right through me.

"I didn't mean to scare you," he says softly. Then he moves me so that my butt is securely anchored on the desk I fell over, drops his arms, and steps back. His eyes are hooded. There's a telltale vein pulsing on the side of his forehead. His heart must be pounding just as hard as mine.

"It's a good question, Tori," he says after the silence has stretched too long. "Why has she decided that you're her target?"

I shake my head, dumbfounded. "I don't know. I've never even seen her before this term."

"We'll have to do some digging. But in the meantime,

we can do some basic sabotage, like shaving cream on her car windscreen, and making a mess in her locker. Stuff that lets her know she's not welcome here."

Her car is her pride and joy. She's one of the lucky ones who has her P plates already and can drive herself to school. It's part of the reason she's so popular.

"How does that help me get the lead role?"

"It doesn't, not directly. But if we can make her life hell, she might just go back to where she came from."

It sounds pretty lame. But then, I guess the whole thing is lame. I couldn't win the audition on my own merits and now I want to steal it from someone else? *Lame.*

It's not just Beauty at stake here, I remind myself. Veronica has come in and stolen my life. She's taken my friends and my spot at the top table. She's set me up to be the person they all pick on. Beauty is just the final straw. I vowed that would never happen to me again.

#NeverEver.

"Okay." I nod decisively. "You do the car and I'll do the locker. Just don't get caught."

He grins. "Don't you get caught either. Or I'll have to come and rescue you again."

18 GLITTER IN THE AIR

It's been two weeks since Cole and I came up with our sabotage plans. Cole's already acted on his with the shaving cream, but all Veronica did was wash it off. *The girls*, that is, Jo, Tiffany, Sarah, and Hillie, all helped her. They looked like they were having *fun*. Not the desired result.

Cole upped the ante the next time by disconnecting some wire under the bonnet. So the car wouldn't start, she called the motor vehicle assistance line, and the girls waited with her. Apart from a minor inconvenience, it wasn't a big deal.

I'm biding my time, waiting for the best chance to do something to her locker. I can't bring myself to do anything too nasty. Nope, no bubble gum, or mud pies, or fake blood for me. I've decided to do a glitter bomb. I'll also put tinsel and confetti through everything.

Hehe. That stuff never comes out.

Cole's already got her locker combination and moved stuff around in it to freak her out. She never even noticed. I thought he might have taken something, like her mirror or a textbook but it turns out he wasn't able to go hardcore and outright steal. Not that I blame him. Low level pranks are one thing, but neither of us want to take it too far. Not yet anyway.

I keep reminding myself why I'm doing this. I want my life back. Not only has Veronica stolen my friends, and my lead role, she undermines me every chance she gets with the teachers. Things I used to take for granted, like being chosen as captain for the debate team, and being on the student council, have gone. Before Veronica came here I would have been voted vice-captain of the school. I don't know how she did it, but she wrangled herself into popularity and when the votes were counted she beat me by a fair margin. I'm trying not to be bitter, but it sucks.

I've convinced myself it isn't too bad like it is. Nothing's *really* changed. I'm still sitting at the same lunch table, I still hang out with the same people, except for rehearsal where it's a different crowd. And sure, nobody talks to me much. But they never did anyway, although they listened to every word I said. Now I don't even have that pressure.

One thing that has changed, and I don't like it. Every single morning, I find myself straightening my hair.

Me! I can't stand it, having to nearly burn myself to get that perfect look. Yet I'm doing it every single morning without fail, just like Veronica and all the other clones.

Gah! I'm a clone!

That's it. It's time to step things up and hold up my end of the deal. It's time to be the glitter fairy.

"WHERE DO you think you're going?"

I freeze. I didn't think Mum would be up so early on a

Tuesday. I'm meeting Cole outside in five minutes, four minutes actually, and I don't have time to talk to Mum if I'm going to get to school early enough to do the thing. The 'thing'. That's what I'm calling it now.

"I'm going to school to do the thing," I say. I roll my eyes at myself for being so vague. Of course, she's going to ask questions.

"And the thing is?" There is it. "You're still grounded, remember."

"It's for the school play." And it kind of is. "I need to get an early start."

Mum thinks about this for a minute, studying me like I'm an insect under her microscope. I must pass inspection because she finally nods.

"Okay, but next time run it past me first."

I swing into the kitchen to grab an apple and a bottle of water from the fridge. No need to skip breakfast now that I don't have to be quiet. "Sure, Mum," I say over my shoulder breezily. Nothing funny going on here, no sir.

"How are you getting to school? Do you need a lift?"

"Um." I *had* been planning to get a ride on the back of Cole's bike. That's two things Mum wouldn't approve of rolled into one big ball of fun. Cole, and motorbikes. "I've got a ride."

"Who with?" She's not going to drop it.

"Cole?" It comes out as a question. It's a pity I can't lie, but she sees through me very time. Unless it's a lie of omission. I kind of rock at those. Not a proud moment.

"Cole." Mum hasn't recognised the name, thank goodness. She's trying though. "Do I know him? And more importantly, what sort car does he drive. I'm not having you get driven around in a death trap."

Which is how it came to be that Mum drove Cole and I

to school. I had to own up about the motorbike and she wasn't having it.

Cole loved it. He knew Mum hadn't figured out that he was the Cole that I knew in primary school, the one that she had taken an instant dislike to. I wasn't going to tell her either. Cole kept his mouth shut, thank goodness. I put him safely in the back seat just in case.

Mum's playing her Pink album as we drive along when the song 'Glitter in the Air' comes on. I glance back at Cole when the song starts, knowing exactly which one it is after listening to this album fifty trillion times. His eyes widen as he hears the chorus and he tries to contain his laughter. No chance. He loses it. A chuckle escapes him, which makes me giggle, and before I know it we're both rolling around on the floor laughing. Not the floor, obviously, but the car seat.

Mum tries to get us to 'calm down' to no avail. She doesn't have a clue about what's set us off. It's just too funny. I mean, it's a slow, serious song and all, but if you forget about the lyrics and focus on the chorus, about glitter in the air.

Well. Enough said.

As the song ends and my giggles finally ease I rub my eyes. They're stinging from the tears mixing with my mascara. I must look a mess. I swing the mirror down from the roof and look.

Yep, a total mess.

"There's baby wipes in the glove box." Mum glances over, taking in my face.

By the time I get myself fixed up using my emergency makeup kit we've arrived at school. I'll have to do a video on that for the young ones. *How to survive makeup emergencies.* When I get my phone back, that is.

"It's awfully quiet," says Mum. There's only one other car in the car park. "Are you sure you've got the right day?"

"We're just a bit early," I say.

"The rest are probably already there," says Cole.

We're both being vague, maybe stretching the truth a little, but we haven't outright lied to her.

"Let me know if you need a ride home."

I'm not sure why she's being so nice, and it makes me uneasy. Especially as I'm still grounded. There's no way she knows Cole's last name, that's for sure. And I intend to keep it that way.

"Thanks for the ride, Mrs Pearson," says Cole politely.

"You're welcome. Have a good day, kids."

"Bye, Mum." I wait until she drives away before turning to go into the quiet school. With a deep breath and clutching my school bag carefully I walk up the path with Cole by my side.

"That was fun," says Cole.

I give him a sharp glance, but he's being serious.

"I thought you said your Mum didn't like me."

"She doesn't. Sorry to burst your bubble, she just hasn't put two and two together and figured out who you are. Don't worry. She will."

"I guess that's something to look forward to, then." Cole smirks. "I'm going to make sure she thinks I'm the golden-haired boy before she remembers that I'm really not."

"Sure. Great idea." I inject as much sarcasm into my voice as I can. "Hang around her so she has more of a chance for her memory cells to kick in. Then she can ban me from hanging out with you, too."

"Now, now, don't worry." Cole slings his arm loosely around my shoulders as we walk. "We're already hanging out without her knowing about it. Even if she does remember I'm pond scum and she doesn't like me, we'll always have the treehouse."

His words make me feel better, as does the warm weight of his arm. I have to hold myself back from snuggling into his side, like a real girlfriend. I'm surprised at how badly I want to.

In the end, doing the booby trap was an anticlimax. Cole kept a lookout while I did the deed. I sprinkled glitter all through her locker, into the pages of her books, and even in the paper bag which held a mouldy sandwich. I set up the 'bomb' by carefully placing my pre-prepared glitter filled tissue-paper- -sphere in the top of the door frame. When she opens her locker it will fall apart, covering her in glitter.

Surprise!

19 FIGHT

"**I** know it was you!"

Veronica is standing five centimetres from my face, pointing her finger and glaring. Seriously, her look could melt an iceberg. It *so* does not go with the glitter in her hair, on her face, her shoulders and even the tip of the finger that's almost poking me.

I take a step back and bite my tongue to keep from laughing. I can't hold it back, a giggle escapes and I put my hand over my mouth.

"You. You," Veronica is sputtering. She's so angry she can't get her words out.

"What's wrong, Veronica?" I say casually. "I didn't get the memo about the sparkly dress code this morning."

"You're going to pay for this, Victoria." She snarls out my name and a flash of fear goes through me at her intensity. I've got no need to worry, right? I mean, what can she do to me? There's no proof it was me.

"Hillie Swan saw you and Cole getting dropped off by your Mum this morning." She steps closer. "*Early* this morning."

"So?" So maybe there's a little proof it was me. But it doesn't mean she knows anything. She's just guessing.

"So?" Veronica's voice is high pitched. "So, you destroyed my locker with your stupid little prank! Like father, like daughter."

"What are you talking about?" A chill goes through me at the mention of my father. What does Dad have to do with this?

"Don't play dumb. You know what he did to me. To my family." She steps in and shoves me, hard. "And I'm going to make you pay."

I stumble backwards, almost going down and but managing to stay on my feet.

Oh no, she didn't.

There's a few kids at the end of the otherwise empty corridor and they start moving towards us. I don't have much time before a teacher arrives, but I'm not going to put up with this.

"You don't get to come in here and steal my life and then act like it's my fault." I launch myself at her and in seconds we're rolling around on the floor clawing at each other.

She grabs my hair and pulls. I screech, and head butt her in the nose. I connect with her forehead instead and it probably hurts me more than her. I'm scrabbling for purchase and get a good chunk of her hair and yank, as hard as I can. She screams. It's a swear word and it's loud. One of her fingernails catches my arm as she flails. They're three-inch manicured talons and it freaking hurts.

A crowd has gathered. I don't realise this until someone grabs me under my arms and tries to pull me off her. She's scratching at me and I fight the grip of the person behind me. Trent Riordan is trying to get hold of Veronica and finally locks his arms around her upper body, caging her in. She's fighting him while still trying to hit me.

I'm being pulled away backwards and her hair slips from my grasp. I've got a some clenched tight in my fist and it comes away with me. She curses again and her hand flies to her head. She's glaring and still screaming threats and insults as she's manhandled away from me. I'm panting, sucking in air in deep gasps. But strangely, I haven't said a word. I've focused all my energy on destroying her physically.

"Easy," says a voice low in my ear.

I go limp as soon as he speaks, the fight rushing out of me with just one word. It's Cole. Of course, it's Cole.

I turn in his arms and burrow my face into his chest. The tears come now. It's just a reaction to the fight, I know this. But I can't seem to stop.

Cole strokes my hair with his hand, his other arm holding me close. He's whispering into my ear, soft, soothing sounds that make me gradually relax.

"It's okay," he says. "I've got you."

"She, she– " I gulp. I'm trying to talk but my voice is coming out in giant hiccupping breaths.

"Ssh," Cole says. "Take a minute. You're lucky, Riordan's got her. She can't get you."

That snaps me out of it. My head comes up and I go stiff in his arms. I'm inches away from Coles' emerald green eyes. "You mean," I say slowly, "*she's* lucky. I can't get *her*."

Cole grins. "Sure, that's what I meant."

He glances at my hair and his grin gets bigger. My eyes narrow.

"You've got a bit of something in your hair." His eyes sparkle. "I don't know, it might be glitter. It's a good colour for you."

I can't stay mad at him. I was never mad at Cole, anyway. It's not his fault I got busted. And it's no surprise I've got glitter in my hair. I look down at myself. Yep. Covered in it. Guess that's what happens when you roll around on the floor with someone who's had a glitter bath.

The strand of blonde hair still clenched in my fist catches my attention. I smile, grimly. I might not have been exactly in the right, but I stood up for myself. It's a good feeling. I wave my fist at Cole. "She's not going to forgive me for this."

"Is that blood?" Cole catches my arm and examines it. It's blood alright, on my arm from where her fingernails dug in.

Cow.

I don't feel so bad about pulling her hair out by the roots, now.

"What's going on here?" The voice comes from behind me. It's the principal. Of course.

Could my day possibly get any worse? You'd think I'd have learned not to ask that question.

I try to make myself as small as possible, huddling in front of Cole. It's no use.

Mr Chapple walks to the middle of the crowd and stands with his hands on his hips as he surveys the students gathered. It's pretty easy to see who the odd ones out are. That would be the two girls covered in glitter and glaring at each other.

Mr Chapple points at Veronica. "You," he says. He turns slowly, eyes searching until they land on me. He points. "And you."

He finishes his survey of the circle then fixes us with a hard stare. "My office. Now."

20 NEW TACTIC

"What have you two got to say for yourselves?"

We're sitting in the principal's office, Veronica and me, having been marched there directly from the scene of our crime.

Mr Chapple is leaning back in his chair with his arms folded. Veronica and I are both perched on the edge of twin chairs, facing the desk. Neither of us say anything.

Mr Chapple sighs. "I don't want to have to call your parents if it's something we can sort out in-house. But I will if I have to."

I look at Veronica. She's looking back, her eyes wide. She gives a minute shake of her head. I agree. I don't want my parents called either. For that moment in time we're both on the same side.

"It was just a stupid prank," I say. "I didn't mean for anyone to get hurt."

"And I overreacted," says Veronica. "I shouldn't have pushed Victoria."

She turns to me. "I'm sorry, okay?"

I nod. "I'm sorry too."

Her hands are clenched on the arms of her seat, knuckles white, as she twists towards me. There's a grim set to her face. She's not enjoying this. I can't say that I am either.

"Alright, girls." Mr Chapple smiles warmly. "It's good that you've taken ownership of your actions, and that you've apologised to each other. I won't have to call your parents in here, after all."

Veronica and I let out twin sighs of relief.

"But," Mr Chapple continues. "Actions have consequences. Otherwise we'd have everybody rolling around in the school halls covered in glitter."

I'm not sure if he's joking or not. I mean, he doesn't seem to be angry. And I think he almost smiled when he said the word 'glitter'. The corner of his mouth twitched. But talk of consequences has me feeling sick in the stomach.

"Yes, Sir," I say.

"Sorry, Sir," says Veronica.

"So here's what we're going to do. And when I say 'we', I mean you." Now he does smile. It's a bit scary. "You're both on lunchtime detention for the next month. You'll be on the cleanup crew for the second half of lunch and I expect you to collect at least one full garbage bag of rubbish from the school grounds." He fixes us with a stern eye. "Each."

A month is a long time. Practically until the end of term. It's going to be a pain, especially as we're in the middle of summer and it's hot as hell. But it's totally doable. And the fact that he said 'each' makes it easier as it means we don't have to do it together.

"And you'll both need to go and see the guidance counsellor."

"What?"

"But, Sir!"

We both speak at the same time and Mr Chapple raises his hand.

"Enough. If you don't like it, I'll bring your parents in and we can discuss a more suitable punishment."

I look down at my hands, defeated. "Yes, Sir."

Veronica mimics my position and my words.

"I'm extremely disappointed in both of you. I expect better of you. You'll both be seniors next year. Look at me, girls."

Our heads rise together.

"This is your first, and final, warning. If there is any of this sort of behaviour again, even a hint of it, then you'll both be suspended. Is that clear?"

We both nod and say, "Yes, Sir,", together. It would be funny, and a little creepy, if it wasn't so serious.

"Good. Now go and get yourselves cleaned up. Tori, you might want to get that scratch looked at by the school nurse. Then get back to class."

We both rise to our feet.

"And girls?" We stop and turn back to him. "Try to get on, please? I know this is difficult for you both, but the sins of the fathers shouldn't get carried on to the next generation. Make a fresh start."

Now I'm plain confused. I don't have a clue what he's talking about, but Veronica seems to. She nods and heads out the door.

"Tori." Mr Chapple's voice stops me before I fully escape. I turn back to him. "This is becoming a pattern with you. Last term with Cassandra Parish, and now with Veronica Mooney. It's time to grow up." He gives me one final hard look, then flicks his hand at the door in dismissal.

"Yes, Sir. Thank you, Sir." I bolt before he can call me back again.

The door slams shut behind me. Whoops. I forgot it's spring loaded. I nearly slam straight into Veronica. She was obviously waiting for me and I hope she didn't hear the principal's final comments.

"Don't think this means we're even," she hisses. She keeps her voice too low for the office ladies to hear. "I'm still going to make you pay."

I watch her walk away, gathering my thoughts. *This is just great.* Not only do I have to look out for Veronica's pay back, for something I'm clueless about, now I've got another secret to keep from my mother. And what did the principal mean about the sins of the fathers?

Right now, the only person I want to see is Cole. Maybe he can help me make sense of all this.

If I'm honest with myself, the only person I've wanted to see for quite some time is Cole. I think I like him. I wonder if he feels the same?

You should ask him. There's that little voice in my head.

Um. No. Because what if he doesn't? The easy camaraderie we've been enjoying would snap in an instant.

But what if he does?

That's the question, isn't it? Because, if he does? Game changer.

Maybe it's time to get brave and find out.

He doesn't fit into my #perfect world, not in any way, shape or form. But he can help me get it back. He *is* helping me get it back. If I succeed, no, *when* I succeed, I'm going to make sure that my world includes Cole. I can't go back to the way things were before. I don't even want to. Things are going to be different when I get back on top. Even if it's not quite #perfect.

21 FAMILY DINNER

Mum turns up at the school gates after school to pick me up.

I'd planned to catch the bus home, so to see her familiar red Prius out the front of the school is a surprise.

"Hi," I say as I climb into the front seat. I'm feeling guilty and wonder if Mr Chapple ended up calling her.

"Hi, sweetie." She leans over to kiss my cheek.

"Eww! Mum!" My reaction is reflex. "Not at school! I'm not five anymore."

Mum smiles across at me. "Well I'm your mother and I love you. So you have to put up with it."

I scowl and cross my arms over my chest, scrunching down in my seat. I'd hoped to catch up with Cole after school. I've only seen him at lunchtime and it wasn't the place for *that* conversation. He did keep me company on my rubbish duties, though.

"What happened to your arm?" Mum asks, spotting the huge Band-Aid the school nurse plastered on me.

"Nothing, it's just a scratch." No more questions, please. "Not that I don't appreciate it, but why are you picking me up?"

"We've got that thing. I forgot to mention it this morning, with all the excitement of meeting Cole." She glances across at me as we idle at a stop sign. "You know, he seems familiar. Have I met him before?"

I shake my head. "Probably, I don't know. What thing?"

"Are you and Cole dating? I was just wondering, because I thought we talked about getting Trent Riordan to ask you out."

"Mum." I grit my teeth. "Enough about Trent, already. He's not my type. Plus, I think he has a girlfriend." I'm counting the fact that he was the one to pull Veronica off me as a sign of romantic interest. Stretching the truth? Maybe. Anything to stop my mother's matchmaking attempts.

"Really? That's a shame, the two of you would have been perfect together. You should have got to him faster." She won't take a hint. And she hasn't answered my question.

"What thing, Mum?" I ask. My voice is a little cool but I can't help it.

"We're meeting Dad for dinner and a movie. Family night, remember?"

Family night. It used to be a thing, once, every Tuesday night. Then Dad got too busy at work, and Mum joined a book club, and it sort of faded away.

"We don't do that anymore. Do we?" Maybe we do now? I'm not sure.

"We're reinstating it. I'm sure we talked about this."

"Can't I go home and get changed first?"

Mum sighs in frustration. "Why do you think I'm picking you up? It saves us half an hour, at least. The bus takes way too long to get you home."

We sit in silence after that. I try to decide if I should tell Mum about the fight, and just wear it. There's not really much else she can do to punish me short of home schooling me. And that would be too much hard work for her. Heaven forbid, she gave up her social life to look after her kids.

Yeah, yeah, Mum works too. But her job is in a high-class clothing boutique, which she loves, and she's only part time. Dad, with his job as a detective in the police force, is our main breadwinner. If it wasn't for Mum's parents help, we wouldn't have our fancy house. You wouldn't know it, looking at my grandparents up in Bonalbo, but they've got money. They believe in living a simple life and they like country the small country town. From what I've gleaned over the years, Gran and Gramps gave Mum and Dad a hefty deposit for our house. They had to borrow to pay off the rest, but it gave them a head start. If anyone looks too closely at our #perfect life they'll see the truth. We're making ends meet, with a little left over, but we're not rich by any standards. Unlike the rest of the people who live in our suburb. But appearances are everything to Mum.

We beat Dad to the restaurant. It's nice. Indian food, my favourite. Dad rushes in about twenty minutes after we get there. Mum is agitated with his late arrival, but trying not to show it. She gets up to greet him and I can see them exchange heated words but can't make out what they're saying.

"What's going on with Mum and Dad?" asks Jenna. "They're acting weird, aren't they?"

I nod. My little sister is perceptive when she wants to

be. There's five years between us and we're not super close, but we get on alright.

"I'm not sure what this is all about," I say. "It's been ages since we had family night out."

"Yeah, I used to look forward to it." Jenna sighs. "Tonight's not going to be fun."

I agree. Mum and Dad come to the table and sit together.

"Well, girls, this is good am I right?" Dad's using his happy jolly voice. The one that says he's playing the part of 'best Dad ever'. It's a mood he sometimes gets in and it usually means he and Mum are fighting.

"What movie are we going to see?" asks Jenna.

Mum and Dad exchange glances.

"Your father has to go back to the station after dinner," says Mum. "But we'll enjoy a nice meal together and then us girls will go and see a movie."

Mum's voice is bright and happy, in a fake sort of way. This is going to be a long night. And I need to find a way to ask Dad what's going on with Veronica Mooney. What did he do to her father that makes her hate me so much?

"How's school?" asks Dad. That's a bad question for me so I let Jenna field it. She rattles on about her classes and her friends and who likes who and some show she's watching on Netflix. She could talk under water, that girl. For once I'm grateful.

"This is nice, right?" Mum says this when Jenna finally draws a breath. We've already ordered, and the food is starting to come out. There's steamed rice for the table, and all the food goes in the middle, so we can share. It *is* nice. Almost perfect, actually. If only Dad didn't have to go back to work. I'm pretty sure that's why Mum and Dad were arguing earlier.

Mum excuses herself to go to the ladies' room and takes Jenna with her. This is my chance.

"Can I ask you something, Dad," I say. He nods.

"I know you can't talk about work or anything, but there's this girl at school and she says you did something to her father. Her name's Veronica Mooney."

"Veronica Mooney." Dad says her name like he knows her. "I didn't know she was at your school."

"She's new this term."

"Is she giving you trouble?" Does he expect her to give me trouble? Maybe I should tell him everything. But no. This is Mum's #perfect family dinner and I don't want to ruin it. News of our fight would definitely ruin it.

"Not really," I say. Besides, it's nothing I can't handle.

"Good. It sounds like she's making a fresh start, but it would be best if you kept out of her way." That seems to be all he's going to say on the matter. I need more.

"What happened with him? Can you tell me anything?"

Dad shakes his head. "You know I can't talk about my work. Just let me know if something happens."

And that's that.

Dad rushes back to work as soon as we finish eating and Mum gets the staff to bundle the leftovers into doggie bags, so we can take them home. Leftovers, yum.

While we're waiting I decide to broach the topic of the play. It's going to come out, and maybe if I'm the one to bring it up I won't be punished as badly.

"Mum, there's something I need to tell you."

Mum looks tired. "What is it?"

"It's about the school play." I hesitate and she focuses all her attention on me.

"I—" I swallow hard. "I didn't get the lead role."

"What do you mean? You had that in the bag."

This is going just as badly as I'd feared. "I stuffed up the audition scene, I played it all wrong. And there's this new girl who did the play at her old school and she nailed it." I shake my head, remembering Victoria's interpretation of the scene. "She was really good, Mum. You should have seen her."

I look up from the napkin I've been shredding to find Mum watching me. Her gaze is sympathetic. Can that be right?

She reaches out and touches my hand, saving what remains of the napkin. "Oh, honey. I know how much you wanted that part."

I've started now, might as well come clean about everything. "I didn't even get to be the understudy. I'm doing costume and makeup. When I went and saw the teacher I was able to convince her to let me be the second understudy, as long as I keep doing the backstage job as well. But it's not like it matters. There's no way something bad would happen to both of them."

"No, it's unlikely." Mum smiles and it catches me off guard. "It will be good for you to be able to enjoy the play without all the pressure, you know?"

"It will?" I have to pinch myself to make sure I'm awake, and this is my mother talking. This is sooo not the reaction I expected. "You're not mad?"

"Mad?" Mum laughs. "Why would I be mad? As long as you're involved somehow it's all good."

"Who are you, and what did you do with my mother?" I tilt my head to the side to look at her. "I thought it was all about being perfect."

"Perfect is good, but only as long as you're happy. I want you to be happy, Tori."

"So I can quit swim squad?" I'm hopeful.

"No." She shakes her head. "I want you to be fit as well as happy. They go together, believe it or not."

I'm dubious but decide not to argue. I'm so relieved I'm not in trouble about missing out on Beauty that I'm almost giddy. "Whatever you say."

The waitress comes back with our wrapped leftovers and we stand to leave.

"Can we skip the movie tonight?" I say. I'm exhausted and just want to go home.

"I've got homework to do," says Jenna. She's on the same page as me.

Mum looks from one of us to the other. "This is meant to be our family bonding time. Your father and I feel like we're drifting apart, as a family. That's why we're bringing back Tuesdays. But if neither of you want to, then there's no point."

Immediately I feel bad. "It's not that we don't want to, it's just that it's a school night. Maybe we should switch nights?"

Jenna is shaking her head behind Mum's back. Too late, I realise that would mean spending Friday or Saturday night with the parents. Lame.

"Or we could do dinner through the week and go to the Sunday movies when it's cheap. Once a month or something." Or once a year would be good too. I keep that thought to myself. Mum's trying to do a good thing for us and I don't want to be the one to wreck it. See, I can be grateful.

"We'll see." Mum sounds tired. "Let's just go home and we can work it out later. It's not the same without your father, anyway."

Jenna and I exchange worried looks.

"It will be alright, Mum." I put my arm around her in a side hug. I haven't hugged my mother for years, but it feels right.

"I know," she says brightly. "It always is."

22 BANISHED

The next day at school everyone is still talking about the fight. I thought it was bad yesterday. But the word has spread even further.

When I walk past two Year Eight girls giggling over their phone I think nothing of it. Then they see me, and their eyes go wide. They nudge each other and whisper.

I narrow my eyes and march over to them.

"What?" I demand.

The tallest girl's eyes flick to the phone in her hand then back to me. She puts her hand behind her back, out of sight. "Nothing."

I hold my hand out. "Give."

She does.

Huh. I didn't think that would work.

There's a video onscreen looping over and over. I don't know the person who posted it, but they've hash tagged it #girlfight and #sparkles and it's got a lot of views.

A lot.

The shot starts from far off and moves closer to the

action. One of those kids I saw at the end of the hall had a phone.

Great.

It shows the whole fight. Veronica shoving me, me launching myself at her, and then both of us rolling around on the floor. It cuts off and loops back to the start just after the boys pull us off each other.

The start of the clip is too far away to make out our faces properly, and by the time the person gets close enough you can only see our backs and hair everywhere. Even the boys' faces can't really be seen. A lucky accident. Anyone who knows it was us would recognise us, but there's a small chance my mum wouldn't realise it's me.

"Thanks," I say, handing the phone back to the girl. I stumble off, feeling numb.

AT LUNCHTIME I'm still in turmoil over the video. I trudge over to our table, head down, not noticing anything else about me. Which is why I don't see the problem before I get there.

There's nowhere to sit. Sure, there's lots of half spaces if people would shuffle along a bit. Once I would have just shoved in and made them all move. Now I'm not so sure of myself. And no-one will meet my eye. Except Veronica.

I feel her gaze on me, and when I look up from my survey of the seating situation she's wearing a nasty smile. My insides clench. This isn't good.

"Well," she drawls. "I'm surprised you'd show your face here after yesterday."

I roll my eyes. "Dramatic much?"

"You're not wanted here, Victoria." She spits out my

name. "The way you keep hanging around us at lunchtime is pathetic."

There's a collective gasp from around the table. Mutterings of "she didn't!", and "oh, my, God,". No one speaks up though. Jo and Tiffany are staring at Veronica like she's a goddess.

"No, you're pathetic." It's lame, but it's the best I can do. My eye catches on her bright red nails. Stick-ons for sure. I rally. "You come in here with your straight hair, and your fake nails and everyone follows along behind the bright new shiny—" I reach for a word insulting enough and nearly slap myself in the face when the word comes out. —thing." I finish strong though. "You're all pathetic!"

There's shocked gasps from around the table. Guess nobody likes being called pathetic.

I turn around to make my dramatic exit, half expecting Cole to be there. He has a way of materialising right when I need him. He's not. The whole lunch room is looking at us though. A few kids have their phones out.

Nothing to see here, guys. I'm leaving.

I stride away. Every step is fast and deliberate. If a storm had legs that would be me. Fury is my name. I power through the door and five steps outside and around the corner. Then I stop. I droop a little. That really took it out of me.

What now?

I look slowly around the quadrangle. There's trees and shade, with tables or benches under each tree. More benches line the sides of the buildings and there's kids everywhere. Looks like there's life outside the cafeteria after all. Who knew?

"Tori!" I search for the voice. It's a girl, faint. A long

way away or not quite loud enough, I'm not sure which. "Over here."

Waving arms catch my attention from under one of the trees. There's a group of kids over there. Some of them are sitting, some of them— boys— are mock wrestling and shoving each other in that physical way boys have. Cavemen. Ugh.

I recognise Cassie and Sam. It's Cassie who called out.

Walking over, I take stock of the other kids. It looks like it's Jack's group. Jack isn't with them, but Scotty's there, as well as Josh, Eli and Jasmine, all their usual gang.

"What's up with you?" Sam raises a questioning eyebrow. We're getting to know each other a bit better the last few weeks at rehearsals and while we're not besties, we tolerate each other. We even get on sometimes. And I could see Cassie becoming a good friend. Which is a bit weird, actually, considering where we were at last term. I saw the blossoming relationship with Jack and Cassie and wanted it for myself. It's not that I wanted Jack, although I'd asked him out. Not a proud moment. But really, I was just after someone who wasn't my mother's choice. Thankfully they've forgiven me, and I've got to the point where I can talk to them and not be thinking about our history all the time. Hopefully, neither are they.

"I've been banished," I say, shrugging. I'm trying to play it cool but in reality I'm still totally pissed off.

Sam's eyebrows almost lift off her head. She whistles.

"Let me guess," says Cassie. "That would be self-proclaimed Queen Veronica."

"Is that what she's calling herself?" I frown. I hadn't heard that. Still, it doesn't surprise me.

"Looks like she's taken over your spot, Tori," Sam observes. "Does that bother you?"

That's Sam. Always straight to the point even if it's inappropriate. I answer her anyway.

"Hell, yes, it bothers me." My voice comes out fierce. It surprises even me. "I haven't done a thing to her, but she's got it in for me. At first, I thought I was imagining things. It was all just bad timing and coincidence. But now—" I trail off, my anger winding down and turning into contemplation. It really does help to get things off your chest. Who knew? Today is a day for learning.

"What's happened now?" asks Sam.

"Well, she banished me, obviously."

We all laugh.

"You're better off without them," says Cassie. "I don't mean to be rude, but your old friends are biatches."

"She's right." A soft voice from beside us. The boys are all goofing off and not paying attention to the conversation, but Jasmine has been quietly taking it all in. "I know they were your friends and all, but you're a different person now. You're a lot nicer."

I smile. "That's a good thing. I've got to take the positives where I can find them."

"What did I miss?" Jack squishes himself in beside Cassie and she snuggles into him. It's cute. I wish I had a boy I was that comfortable around, but I'm not jealous anymore.

I miss Cole.

"Tori." Jack nods at me. "You don't normally hang with us. What gives?"

Is his voice cool? Or am I overanalysing. I miss Cole even more. Jack's eyes flick to something behind me and he grins.

Warmth at my back, and that tantalising smell make me think I've conjured my gorgeous boy. An arm goes around my upper chest, stretching from shoulder to shoulder, and I'm pulled back into a hard body.

"Hi." A voice at my ear. I did conjure him. "You okay?"

Goose bumps travel from my neck down my arms. I'm not sure we're the sort of friends who touch like this, but I'd like to be. So bad. Cassie and Sam are watching us with interest. Jack now has his arm around Cassie and says something softly to her. She giggles and blushes. At least that's one less set of eyes on me.

I twist so I can see Cole's face and his arm falls away.

"Did something happen?" His eyes are so green this close, but I can see the concern in them.

Don't get distracted by the pretty eyes, Tori.

I nod, but my words escape me.

"She got banished by the new Queen Vee," says Sam. "We've taken pity on her though. She's our biatch now."

I want to be offended but I just can't. Sam's tone is so dry, but I can tell she's trying to make light of things, so I don't have to tell the story again. Or maybe they've adopted me? There could be worst things.

23 WATER BABY

The bell rings for us to go back to class and everyone starts getting up. This lunchtime has turned out to be a good one. Getting banished had a silver lining. The gang has welcomed me, and Cassie said quietly that I can hang out with them whenever I want. I'm still thinking about that, but it's nice to have a backup option.

Apparently, Cole is already one of the guys, news to me but there you go. Once Cole and Jack were filled in on what had happened, talk turned to their latest indoor soccer game. Most of the guys and Cassie and Sam are in a team together. It sounds like a lot of fun.

I pick up my bag and turn to go to class, but Cole stops me with a hand on my arm. He pulls me onto the bench beside him. "Stay a minute."

The crowd quickly clears and when it's just the two of us he speaks. "Do you want to skip this afternoon?"

I stare, aghast. "Because that went so well for me last time."

He rolls his eyes. "You're not going to get busted twice in a row."

"Not sure I want to take that chance. I've almost finished being grounded from last time. I don't think I could take any more."

He makes puppy-begging face at me. "Come on, I want to take you surfing."

"You do?" My insides light up at the thought. "I've always wanted to learn to surf. Always."

"I know," says Cole. "I've seen how much of a water baby you are. You're the body surfing pro. So why haven't you ever gone out on a board?"

I sigh. "Mum. Surfing doesn't fit with her list of 'perfect' activities for a young lady."

"So, come with me this afternoon. I've got my board stashed at my mate's beach hut. I've even got a spare wetsuit for you. It's an old one of his sister's."

I so badly want to do this. I love the water and I'm the original water nymph. In my own mind, anyway. But I can't. I shake my head. "Sorry. The answer's no. I can't skip school again, I just can't."

"Come on, live a little. We've only got study hall this afternoon, it's not like they'll miss us."

"*You* might only have study hall." I shake my head. "*I've* got to go and see the guidance counsellor."

"Oh."

"Yeah, oh. Or did you forget about the fight?"

"No way. That was awesome!" He grins, huge. "But I'm going to have to show you how to throw a punch properly for next time."

It's my turn to roll my eyes. "There's not going to be a next time. Jeez. And if my mother ever finds out about *this* time she's going to kill me. Like, for real."

There's still secrets I'm keeping from my mother, like the fact that Cole's sleeping in the treehouse. But I'm not thinking about that right now. I've got to see the guidance counsellor and stop her from phoning my mother.

"Well, if you won't skip with me, and you're not grounded any more, does that mean you can come hang out after rehearsals next week?"

"Maybe. What did you have in mind." Is he asking me out on a date? I think I like that idea.

"Jack and the guys are going out for pizza. Cassie and Sam and Jasmine will be there too. Cassie wanted to ask you, but I told her you were still grounded."

"Oh." I'm disappointed. I mean, it's nice that Cassie thought of me, but it would be better if it was Cole.

"Hey." He touches me lightly on the shoulder. "I was going to ask you to come. But I thought you were still grounded too."

"Oh," I say. It's amazing how different the word can sound with two different meanings behind it. This time it's hopeful. "Are you asking me out, Cole Black?" I try to sound playful, but he can probably sense my desperation. I'm not desperate. I'm just trying too hard. Nope, that's not any better.

Cole grins. It's like he can read my mind. "I didn't do a very good job of it, did I? I don't date much."

"So, this is a date?" I'm still cautious. But optimistic. Cautiously optimistic.

"Yeah, Tori, it's a date. Not super romantic seeing as the whole gang will be there, but I think of you as my girl and I'd like to make it official." His cheeks have gone slightly pink. Is he embarrassed? Wow, it's kind of sweet.

I realise I haven't answered his question and smirk.

Nice that he's the one off balance for a change. "Well—" I say.

"Come on, Tori." He groans. "Don't leave me hanging here. If you don't see me like that then just tell me."

"Okay, I'll tell you."

His face closes down, and he stands, about to walk off. Whoops. Too far.

"Hey!" I grab his arm. "Give me a minute."

"What?" He's almost hostile.

"Jeez, settle down. Come on. Sit here." I put pressure on his arm to pull him onto the bench beside me. Reluctantly, he sits. I take a deep breath and look him right in the eyes.

"Cole, I'd love to be your girl. Truth is, I already think of you as mine. And I miss you when you're not around." Now it's my turn to go pink. I can feel the heat rising in my cheeks.

A slow smile lights up his face. "Really?" he asks, totally serious.

"Really," I reply, equally as serious.

"Good, great. That's great." He scrubs his hand through his hair, then pins me with those brilliant green eyes. "Don't think I'm going to forget how mean you were just now."

"Mean? It's payback for you asking me on our first date with a whole bunch of randoms."

"If we're going to get technical, I think our first date was actually weeks ago in your treehouse. That's when it started for me. I liked you already, but that was the night we started to talk. Really talk. That was the night you let me see the real you. And I realised the girl I knew when we were younger was still in there, and I still liked her."

"Wow." I don't know what else to say to that. Then I do know. "That was the night I first realised how much I still liked you, too. And it's good that we're going out with a group. My mother would never let me go with just you, especially not on a school night."

"Alright, so it's settled." His grin seems to be permanent.

"Yep, it's settled." I sigh. "Now I've got to go and see the guidance counsellor." Which sucks. But my bad day just got a whole lot better. I think I can cope.

24 THIS AND THAT

The session with the guidance counsellor was a drag.

The first ten minutes were a speech she'd obviously rehearsed about how concerned she is about me, and the fight.

"This isn't the first time you've fought with other girls, Tori. Although it didn't get physical with Cassie. I'm concerned that you're having trouble connecting with your peers. I don't want to see this escalate any further."

I fight an eye roll. "The thing with Cassie was all a big misunderstanding. We get on fine now. In fact, we're in the play together. We're even going out for pizza after rehearsal on Monday night."

"Oh. Well. That's good then." She fidgets with her pen, then picks it up and makes a note. I can't read what it says, not for lack of trying.

"And this week's fight with Veronica? Was that a misunderstanding too?"

Now I'm fighting my hands, forcing them to relax

instead of forming into fists. Think calm and happy, calm and happy. "That wasn't my fault. She started it."

"Really, Tori? I don't think that's an excuse. You could have walked away." Her eyes narrow. "And I believe it was you who put glitter all through her locker."

My grin escapes before I can stop it. "It was so pretty."

"Tori—" She's tapping her pen on the desk, impatient or anxious, I can't tell.

"Sorry, Miss. It was a practical joke and she took it all wrong. Then when she pushed me, I don't know. I pushed back."

I look up and meet her eyes, so she knows I'm serious. "It won't happen again."

She sighs. "Alright. But if we have another incident I'm going to have to call your parents. Understood?"

"Yes, Miss. I'd really prefer if you didn't involve them. My mother has a habit of overreacting."

Miss Miller has been the victim of my mother overreacting before and knows exactly what I'm talking about.

"I know. I don't want a repeat of the uniform incident."

I'd forgotten about that one. It was a year or so ago and I'd had the bright idea to create a zigzag hem on my uniform skirt. It was awesome. And extreme. Parts of the skirt were skimming my backside and other parts were longer than my knees. You couldn't see panties or anything, I'd made it all flowy with a lighter material sewn in to cover the gaps. I made it in sewing class, but I don't think our teacher expected me to model it in front of the whole school after I finished it.

The school didn't approve, and my mother got a phone call. She came storming up, took one look at me, and started yelling. I got grounded that time too. The yelling happened in front of Miss Miller, which my mother later apologised for. But she wasn't embarrassed. Nope. I'd done the wrong thing and that was all there was to it.

We finish up our guidance session with Miss Miller extracting a promise from me to 'think before you act'. I'll probably have to go to a follow-up session with her, but for the moment she's just keeping an eye on me. *Phew.*

$\approx$

I'M STILL GROUNDED all weekend but on Sunday afternoon Mum calls me in to 'have a chat.'

"You've done your time," she says. She hands me my phone. "And you've proven yourself to be responsible. You can have this back, and provided you check with me first you can go out with your friends."

I clutch my phone tightly. I'm going to have a million notifications. And I can finally do the new makeup videos for emergency situations. Hannah will appreciate that one, for sure. I've got other ideas too, things I wish I'd known when I first started doing my makeup.

Mum's waiting for a response. I mumble a thankyou and then turn to the important part of the conversation.

"You said I can go out with my friends?" I give her my best puupy dog eyes. "About that—"

Mum raises an eyebrow.

"Can I go out for pizza on Monday night after rehearsal? There's a group going, and they invited me along."

"You didn't waste any time, did you? Who's going?"

"Mum! You don't have to give me the third degree."

"Do you want to go?" she asks. A second eyebrow joins

the first and she looks a bit demented. Why does she have to be like this?

"It's not a big deal. It's just some kids from the play. Cassie, Sam. Cole's going too."

"Cassandra Parish? I know her grandmother from the bakery." Her gaze turns thoughtful, the eyebrows finally returning to their normal place on her face, thank goodness. "What about Tiffany and Jo?"

I shake my head. I didn't think she paid that much attention to my social life. "I don't hang out with them as much nowadays."

"Mmm." Her eyes narrow. "And Cole? The boy next door? What's going on there? He seems like a nice young man."

Mum's driven us to school a couple of times now, and Cole even came over one afternoon, and we did homework together, sitting at the dining room table. Being grounded, I wasn't allowed to go out, but apparently him being at our place was okay as long as we were studying in plain sight. Cole's always on his best behaviour with Mum.

"Umm," I say. I don't want to tell her, but she's going to find out anyway. It all comes out in a rush. "We're kind of dating, but it's still really new. Not that we've actually gone on a date, yet, what with me being grounded and all. Monday night will be the first time and we're going in a group so don't embarrass me, please."

Mum laughs. "Oh, Tori. As if I'd do that!"

She totally would.

"I'm glad you're telling me. Just keep me informed and it's all good." She sighs. "I know this last five weeks has been hard on you, but there was a reason I grounded you. I wanted you to realise how serious your actions are. There's consequences for everything you do. I think you've learned your lesson."

Oh boy. I'm going to be in so much trouble if she finds out the truth about Cole. Or is it just a matter of time? I hope not. It's kind of nice talking with Mum like this. She's way too nosy, but still. It's nice.

"Yes, Mum," I say. "Actions and consequences. Got it."

MONDAY AFTERNOON ROLLS AROUND and with it comes rehearsals. Cole has upped his game in the sabotage department. He slipped a frog into Veronica's bag last week and she screamed like a baby when it jumped out on her. Of course, Trent was the big hero and rescued her from it. I don't know how it's supposed to help me get my role back, but if bad things keep happening to her at rehearsals then maybe she'll get the hint.

Tonight, he got there early and replaced the makeup with a bronzer/self tanner. They're both in the same kind of container and he switched the label and traded places, so the bronzer had the the dewy peach base label and sat in the spot the dewy peach normally sits. Of course, Veronica has been very particular about having 'her' makeup kit in a separate area to everyone else. She wanted her own dressing room, but we don't have the facilities to do that. We think ourselves lucky to have a separate change room for boys and girls. And the makeup is all in together.

We don't normally do the full makeup, but Miss wanted to test it out to get ready for our dress rehearsal. It was perfect timing.

It's a miracle nobody noticed when they were doing her face. Thank goodness I don't have to do her. I was working on Scotty which is a lot of fun. The biggest surprise to me when I started doing theatre was the white dot that goes on the side of your nose, right next to your eyes. It looks stupid up close, but when you're on stage it makes your eyes stand out to the audience. A trick of the light.

Anyway, she got out on stage and the bronzer kept developing. Her face kept getting darker and darker. Miss kept asking for more light. Eventually one of the girls realised what was going on.

"What the hell?" Veronica was pissed. She ran from the stage and to the bathroom to try to scrub it off. It was hilarious. She tried water, then makeup remover and it didn't work. She even tried soap. No luck there either. In the end she went home early, almost in tears. I felt a bit bad, then. I can tell Cole did too. It's going to take a week for it to wear off on its own.

Miss is not impressed.

"This has got to stop," she says. "I don't know who is pulling these pranks but enough is enough."

Nobody admits to knowing anything, although I'm sure some of the guys have been pulled into Cole's schemes. The fake script was classic. They all played along with it and had Veronica convinced that Miss had handed out a new version of the script. Scotty and some of the other guys 'helped' her practice. She had to learn all these new lines before the next rehearsal.

She was so proud of herself when she nailed them all, and then confused when Miss was unimpressed.

Nobody could remember where the new script had come from. Either they all clueless, or Cole had convinced them to prank her. None of the guys were talking.

There were other minor things, like tying shoelaces

together, and moving things to the opposite side of the room to where they were left.

Juvenile. But effective.

But is it going to be enough?

25 DATE NIGHT

After everything settles down and Miss finishes telling us all off, which didn't work, everyone thought it was hilarious, we finally escape.

Cole has borrowed his mother's car for the night and drives us to the Pizza Hut in town. We've got Sam and Scotty with us. Jack and Cassie have gone in his car.

"Who do you think it was?" Sam asks. She's sitting behind me and has grabbed the back of my seat to pull herself forward, so she can talk to us.

I shrug. "I don't know. They've got a great sense of humour, though."

Scotty snort laughs. "I'll say. Evil genius level. Wish I'd thought of it."

Cole is keeping quiet. Maybe it wasn't him? Nah, it was. He just doesn't need the credit.

"You'd think Veronica would take a hint, you know. It's pretty obvious someone doesn't want her there." Sam hits me on the shoulder. "Do you think it's Talia? She's the one who would benefit most. If Veronica quits, she gets to step up into lead."

Cole and I exchange a look. Talia is lovely and doesn't need Sam on her case.

"Nah," I say. "Talia's too nice."

"I heard she might have to quit the play," says Scotty. "Her family is planning a trip to Europe for the Christmas holidays and her parents want to pull her out of school a few weeks early. Which would mean she'd be in Paris when we're doing our last couple of shows."

"Really?" This is good news. "Do you think they'll do it?"

Scotty shrugs. "Dunno. But maybe that's why Miss made you second understudy."

"Far out! I'd better start learning my lines, just in case."

Sam scoffs. "As if you don't know them already."

She's right, I do know them. "Yeah," I admit. "But I haven't been rehearsing."

As a matter of fact, I've almost given up on ever getting my role back. I've been in a bit of a funk about it. The sabotages aren't working, and I feel like I'm going to have to come clean with my mother and deal with the consequences. I mean, how bad could it be? Then I remember how long I was grounded for last time. Yeah, it could get bad.

We pull into the car park and all get out.

"See you in there, slow poke!" Sam rushes off, chasing after Cassie and Jack who pulled in moments ahead of us and are already heading inside. Typical Sam, a hundred miles a minute. But it gives me a moment with Cole.

Scotty and Cole exchange a meaningful look and then Scotty ambles after Sam. I turn to follow, but Cole catches my arm and turns me to face him. He's leaning against the bonnet of his car, all nonchalant and cool.

"Are you okay?" he asks.

I nod. "Yeah, I'm alright. It just feels a bit weird to be out and about after being grounded for so long."

"I meant about the play. You're not giving up, are you?"

"What are you, a mind reader now?"

He shrugs. "No, but I know you. I can tell you're stressing out over this."

"She's not going to quit, Cole. No matter how many times we prank her."

"That's not the attitude, Tori." He reaches out and grips my shoulder. "We're halfway there. Talia is already out of the picture. There's no way her parents will pay all that money to go to Europe for just six weeks. They've got family over there. They'll pull her out of school early, you'll see."

I roll my eyes and shrug off his hand. "I guess."

Cole reaches for me again. This time he grasps both my shoulders and pulls me into his chest. His arms go around me, and I settle into his hug. It feels good, right. He feels good. More than right. I snuggle my head into his neck and wrap my arms around his waist. This is nice.

Then the mood changes as Cole dips his head down to my ear. "Tori," he says. "I don't want to freak you out, but everyone is inside staring out the window, watching us."

I feel my face heat and my arms tighten involuntarily around his waist. I burrow my head into him, trying to hide.

He chuckles, the sound rumbling through me. "Don't think that's going to work."

Then he moves us. He switches our positions so that I'm up against the car and his body is shielding me from onlookers. I yelp as we swing around, my head coming up. He's grinning. "That's better. Think they'll get the hint?"

I peek over his shoulder and see them all still looking. "Nope. Nice try though. We should go in."

Cole growls. Actually growls. "No way. I've got you right where I want you and we're doing this."

"Wow, so romantic."

His eyes have gone dark and I can feel his heart pounding. It matches mine. Is he going to kiss me? I really want him to kiss me. I lean into him more, the pull like gravity. His head dips and his mouth brushes mine and all the words fly out of my head.

"I try," he says, his mouth barely moving.

Then he kisses me. For real, and to hell with who's watching.

I've been kissed before, of course. But I've never experienced anything like this. It's like my head is exploding, in a good way. I've got fireworks going off, starting at my mouth and racing all through me. His lips are soft yet firm. Dancing around my mouth, teasing yet demanding. There's butterflies in my stomach, stirred up by all the fireworks no doubt. And then his tongue touches mine and all the rest was just a buildup, sparklers. Now there's fireworks. The big bangers are going off and my head is spinning. I clutch Cole tighter, giving back every bit as good as I get. Who knows, maybe he's got fireworks too.

Eventually, forever and yet no time at all, he pulls back. He kisses the corner of my mouth, both sides, then rests his forehead on mine. He's breathing heavily. So am I.

"Wow," he says, softly.

"Wow," I repeat. That was some kiss.

We stay like that for several long moments, wrapped together, and I'm soaking it in. Finally, he stirs. His hand pushes my hair back behind my ear and smooths it.

"We better go in," he says.

I'd forgotten about the peanut gallery. I peek over his shoulder. Yep, still gawking.

I nod. I have no more words right now. Cole chuckles, low and throaty, then steps back. My arms fall to my side and I gaze up at him adoringly, a silly smile on my face. I can't help it. Just *wow*. He adjusts his jeans and gives himself a little shake.

"Wow," he says again.

Then he puts his arm around me and walks me in.

Our friends, and I guess they're becoming my friends too, turn around quickly and pretend they weren't staring out the window like it was a movie screen and all they needed was popcorn.

We walk in and Cole's arm falls away. I miss him instantly, but he immediately grabs my hand and entwines our fingers together and I can breathe again.

Our friends pay out on us when we get to the table, but they're good natured about it.

"Took you long enough, mate," says Scotty.

Cassie smiles at me and Sam leans close and gives me a subtle high five. "You go, girl," she says.

All night Cole doesn't leave my side. He's in a very touchy, feely mood. I guess it *is* our first date. And having it happen in a group like this is a good thing. There's no awkward silences. We laugh and joke and I realise, halfway through, that I'm having fun. These are good people, great friends, and a lot of fun. It's hard to believe I thought so badly of them last term. I wasn't a very nice person back then. At least I'm aware of it now, and I'm trying to change.

26 LOOMING DEADLINE

Saturday afternoon is a treat. Martha has finally started her Zen yoga class and I've convinced Cassie and Sam to come with me. I'm unbelievably excited about it. It's been way too long since I did a class.

Jasmine had something else on so she's not with us. I really like Jasmine. I can't believe I used to think she was stuck up, just because she's quiet. I've been sitting with their group all week at lunchtime and it's been nice. Better than nice.

But it doesn't feel right. They've welcomed me, but their friendships go back to primary school and let's face it, I was a complete biatch to them, Cassie especially, up until a few months ago. So, while I'm there, and grateful to have somewhere to go after being evicted by my former friends, it still doesn't feel entirely comfortable.

I'm hoping the yoga class will help that. We can bond.

I would have taken Tiffany and Jo before Veronica came to town. Not sure if they would have liked it, but they would have come with. All the girls would have. I'd have asked Martha how many of us she could handle and then picked who could come and who couldn't out of the other girls in the group. I'd have been nice about it. Wouldn't I? It's hard to admit to myself, but maybe not.

We're sitting on our mats waiting for class to start. The town hall is the venue. It's got a new roof and a paint job since last time I was here, which was the roof fundraiser. That was when Jack put his heart on the line and sang the song he'd written to Cassie. And Cassie's cupcakes took off after that when she won a place in the next round of some cooking competition. In Sydney. Oh, that's right, she ended up winning the whole damn thing and is going to France over the Christmas holidays.

Sam nudges Cassie's shoulder. "Remember that exercise class we did here?"

Cassie giggles. "And your aunt was here giving me dirty looks for being so uncoordinated."

"Then Jack dinked you on his bike and you guys crashed."

"Dinked?" I haven't heard that word before.

"Sheltered childhood, Tori?" Sam rolls her eyes.

"It's doubling. I sat on the handle bars of the bike while Jack was riding." Cassie smiles ruefully. "It didn't end well."

She turns back to Sam and they keep reminiscing about all the 'Yes's' Cassie did last term. I'd heard about her challenge. I thought it sounded a bit silly, but she got the guy so it all worked out in the end.

Meanwhile I've got my own challenge. It's only two weeks until opening night. I've been racking my brain about how to get Veronica to drop out, so I can step in and save the day. Despite all the things we've thrown at her, she won't quit. I mean, why would she? It would take something like a broken leg for her to pull out this close. And that's not something I could arrange, even if I wanted to. It feels like it would be too far.

I sigh, then spend the next hour nicely distracted by our class.

Martha *is* the Zen goddess. She gives us a visualisation to do during the meditation. First, she quotes Walt Disney - 'All our dreams can come true, it we have the courage to pursue them.'

"Walt Disney said this," says Martha. "And it was certainly true for him. He's left a legacy."

She smiles. "But your dreams don't have to be huge, or earth changing. There should be no pressure. Finding your Zen can be as simple as painting or writing and getting consumed in the creative flow. Enjoying nature. Sharing a beautiful, nourishing meal with loved ones. Laughing with friends. The smell of a rose. Even the simple routine of washing the dishes or making your bed can help you be centred."

She looks around the room, meeting the eyes of each person there. "As we do our meditation I want you to visu-alise the simple things that give you pleasure. I'll guide you at the start. You can close your eyes or focus your gaze on the flame." She lights the candle she has set in front of her, then gently taps the cymbal she has to one side, indicating the start of the meditation.

I close my eyes and visualise the things she says. My favourite colour, a rain drop on a window pane, the smell of a rose, my mother's face, the feel of the sun on my face in the early morning, the place I love to go to enjoy nature. That's the beach, for sure. My mind wanders as I remember Cole's offer to teach me to surf. Which makes me think of Cole.

Never did I ever think I'd be dating him. A shiver goes

up my back and goose bumps prickle my arms. He's not even here and he has that effect on me. He's so damn sexy. And sweet and considerate, completely unexpected. Nobody else gets to see that side of him except me.

He's cocky as hell. And oh boy, his body. I love the feel of his arms around me, and the way he holds my hand. It makes me all gooey inside.

If there's one silver lining with Veronica coming to town and taking over my life, it's this. Even living beside me, we wouldn't be this close. Hell, the first night I found him in my treehouse I would have yelled blue murder and Dad would have come and kicked him out. No, it would have been Mum.

He's still sleeping up there a lot of nights. I can't get out to see him every night, but I sometimes see the flicker of torchlight and I know he's up there. I'd know by the yelling next door, anyway. Those are the nights he needs to escape.

I wonder what everyone at school would think if they knew. Nothing good. No, that's Cole's secret and there's no way anyone is finding out.

～

"YOU DIDN'T GO with the girls?" Martha is placing the spare rolled-up yoga mats into a large duffle bag. Cassie and Sam have taken off to meet the others for milkshakes.

"Um, no." I was invited, but still feel like the outsider. They don't do it deliberately, but it's like the chat-fest before class. I just don't have that history with them. Or I do, but it's nothing positive.

"It was a great class today." I'm trying to change the subject.

She smiles. "Thanks, I think it went well."

I begin gathering the foam blocks and putting them into another bag.

"Is there something you wanted to talk to me about, Tori?" asks Martha. "You seem like you've got something on your mind."

Damn Martha, she's way too perceptive. Way better than the guidance counsellor, that's for sure.

"Not really."

"Mmm." Martha gives me a thoughtful look. "How are you getting on with Cassie and Sam? It looks like you've made up after your fight that first day of rehearsal."

"Oh, I didn't think you'd heard that." It shouldn't surprise me, but she hadn't let it show at the time.

Martha chuckles. "Give me some credit. But I was young once, and I know what it's like trying to find your place with your peers."

"I guess we're okay." I shrug. "I never hung out with them before this. I was in a different group."

"Ah, yes. The girls Veronica seems to have wrapped around her finger." Martha frowns. "I heard about the wrestling match between the two of you the other day and I have to say it surprised me. I didn't think I'd ever hear your name linked to something like that."

My face heats and I know I've turned bright red. I feel ashamed of myself. If Martha only knew the truth about what's been going on she'd be so disappointed in me. She can't ever find out. It would be worse than if Mum found out.

"I, uh, I—" I'm stuttering, not really knowing how to respond.

Martha puts a hand on my shoulder and looks me in the eyes. "It's okay, Tori. I'm not judging you. It is what it is. Just remember, you get what you give." She smiles, her eyes warm. "And Karma has a way of sorting things out in the long run."

I think that's supposed to make me feel better, but it makes me feel even worse. I feel a flash of fear. Karma is going to get me, big-time. I just don't know whether it will be for the lying, the sabotage, or for acting like a biatch to everybody. Although, maybe missing out on my lead role was Karma's retaliation for being a biatch.

If I don't want my lies to come out, I'm running out of time to fix it. I've got to find a way to get Veronica to give me back my lead role, my friends, and my life. And the best way to do that is to find out what she's hiding.

I have to talk to Cole.

27 CLUES

"**Y**ou're my final hope. Tell me you've found something."

We're sitting up in the treehouse the next afternoon. Cole's got my laptop and is 'investigating' Veronica. I'm too frustrated with the whole thing, so I'm lying on my belly with my sketchbook in front of me, drawing to try and de-stress. It's the first time I've felt comfortable enough to pull it out in front of Cole. I won't let him look at it yet. Too embarrassing. But he can see the picture I'm working on now.

It's a dreamscape. Something out of *Beauty and the Beast*, the Disney version. Well, not quite the Disney version. My version has a horror movie twist.

There's the huge dining hall with the cups and teapot flying around and dancing with the butler dude. Beauty is sitting sweetly at the table, captivated, totally innocent. I've kept the background dark and sinister looking. In the shadows you can almost see the bad things. Red eyes peering from beneath a chest of drawers. The outline of a hooded figure lurking in the shadows at the foot of the stairs.

A bat with creepy red eyes and sharp teeth hanging upside down from the chandelier. Beauty is oblivious to it all.

Yes, it's dark. But it matches my mood. I feel like it's all about to come crashing down on my head and I'm only a little less unaware than Beauty.

"Give me a minute," says Cole. "Sheesh. I don't have much to go on. You sure you don't know her parents' names? Or where she lived before she moved here?"

"Nope. Dad knows something, though. He recognised her name and told me he couldn't discuss work." I frown. "Mr Chapple as good as confirmed it. He said something about the sins of the fathers not being passed down to the next generation."

"What if your dad arrested hers?" asks Cole. "I'm pretty sure I heard that she lives with her mum. No Dad around. That might explain it."

"But why would that make her hate me? If that's what happened, then he's just doing his job."

Cole gives me a look.

"Yeah, I know. But it wasn't personal. And if her Dad was doing something wrong then he should get arrested."

"Bingo!" Cole turns the computer screen around to face me, showing me a headline before pulling it back so he can keep reading. The glimpse I caught of the headline didn't look good. Drug dealer busted. There was a photo too.

I drag myself up to sitting, flipping my sketchbook shut and pushing it aside. Beauty can wait. This is way more important.

I shuffle over to sit beside Cole, so I can read over his shoulder. He whistles. "Oh, boy. This is definitely personal."

I scan the picture first. There's a man in jeans and a leather jacket with his hands cuffed behind his back. He's being led away by two uniformed police officers. In the background there are several other people. One of them looks very familiar. I look to Cole to find him watching me closely. Then I touch the screen with my thumb and index finger and drag them outward to expand the shot so I can see more detail. Got to love a touch screen.

As the faces in the background get larger I know without a shadow of doubt. That's my father. He's dressed in matching jeans and a leather jacket. But he's not in cuffs, oh no. He's got a badge clipped to his jeans pocket and is holding a stack of papers loosely in one hand.

Cole double taps the screen to bring it back to the original size. "See here?" He points to the second paragraph of the article. "It says it was an undercover operation. The police operative got close to the criminal and his family over a period of two years while gathering enough evidence for the arrest."

He meets my eyes. "Two years, Tori. That's a long time. You'd gain someone's trust in that time."

I nod. "And then, when they turned on you, it would be natural to feel betrayed and want to make them pay."

I sigh and rest my head on Cole's shoulder. He lifts his arm and puts it around me, pulling me close. I'll read the article, I just need a minute.

"I didn't think your Dad was undercover," says Cole. "Isn't he just a normal cop?"

I shake my head. "I don't really know. He comes home every night, so it's not like he was one of those deep undercover cops who disappear for years to get close to the bad guys."

I think back over the last few years. "Honestly? I didn't notice anything different. He's at work, like, a lot. And he and Mum are always fighting about it. That's why Mum brought back 'family dinner.'"

"Family dinner? You don't eat every night?"

I poke him in the stomach and he catches my hand, holding it in his warm grip. "Funny," I say. "When I was little we used to go out to dinner and a movie once a week. Then it stopped, maybe two years ago?"

"Which is when this undercover gig started." Cole's thumb is making small circles on my palm. It's sending tingles through me and I blink hard and pull my hand away. There's time for that later. Right now, I need to focus.

"Yeah, I guess." I frown. "And we started to do them again a few weeks ago. Dad came for dinner, but we never made it to the movie 'cos he had to go back to work. That was the night I asked him if he knew Veronica."

I transfer the computer from Cole's lap to mine, so I can read the article. There's not a lot of detail.

"It says that the undercover operative was posing as a corrupt cop. That would have been easy for Dad, no need for dreadlocks and a new name."

Cole chuckles. "You watch way too many movies, Tori. I don't think you need dreadlocks to be undercover."

I elbow him. "I know, I was joking."

I read on. "Over the period of two years the operative became close to the suspect and his family, including his children. The initial contact was made while the operative was coaching the daughter's baseball team."

I look up, indignant. "Dad never coached my baseball team!"

"You don't play baseball."

I don't. I do everything else, but never was good at ball sports. Fortunately, Mum didn't push it. She just made me pick something else, which is how I started swimming. Poor

Jenna got roped into swim squad too, a few years later to help with her asthma.

"That's not the point," I say. "He was there with her, when he should have been home with his own family. No wonder Mum was pissed with him."

"My dad was a cop." Cole draws his knees up to his chest and wraps both his arms around them. My shoulders feel the loss, but I ignore it as he continues to talk. "Is a cop, I should say. That's why my parents got divorced in the first place."

"Cole." It's my turn to put my arm around him. Which is weird. He's so much bigger than me and I can't reach all the way around him. It's the thought that counts, though. He leans into me. "I didn't know."

"No-one does. I don't talk about it. He got transferred away to Perth, the other side of the country, and I don't see him. Mum got full custody and he didn't fight it." He sounds bitter. "And now I get to put up with Mum and her poor attempts to *find a man*."

"So, you haven't heard from your Dad at all?"

He shakes his head. "Christmas and birthday." He laughs, a forced sound. "I'll give him that much. Every year without fail he rings me on those two days. And he gives me money." He huffs out a laugh. "I thought he was being a cheap arsehole, sending me twenty bucks twice a year. But when I turned sixteen he sent me an ATM card and instructions to go down to the bank with my ID. He'd set up a separate bank account for me. I had to go to the bank to get identified on my own. He didn't even come over to help me do that." He shakes his head again, then smiles. "He must have been putting money into it for years. That's how I was able to buy my bike."

"I wondered about that." He's had his bike ever since he got his Ls, over a year ago. Long before the Lotto win.

"Mum was super pissed. She thought the money should have gone to her seeing as she was the one who had to feed and clothe me."

"Your Dad didn't pay child support?"

"No, he did. She just wanted more." He sneers. "The Lotto win couldn't have gone to a nicer person."

"Cole!" I'm shocked. "You can't say that about your mum! She might not have made good life choices, but she's still your mother."

"Not everyone has a family like yours, Tori." He turns to face me, shrugging my arm away. "They might have problems, but your parents work on them. Family dinner? I never got that. All I got was one trashy boyfriend after the other."

"Cole—" I don't know what else to say but hope he can hear my sympathy in my voice.

"It's okay. It is what it is." The gold in his green eyes sparkles in the light. "I came to terms with it years ago. Why do you think I'm sleeping out here?"

He gestures around my treehouse, with his yoga mat and sleeping bag tucked neatly in their box.

"I thought it was because of the fighting."

"It is, mainly. But I also need space, some peace. I get that out here."

"Should I go and leave you to your peace and quiet?"

He reaches out and grabs my hand. "No. You're the reason for my peace. You give me that, Tori."

My inner Zen goddess must be rubbing off on the outside me. I duck my head, embarrassed. He reaches out to tilt my chin up, making me meet his eyes.

"Thankyou."

Then he dips his head close and kisses me, soft and sweet.

It's just what I need.

Even if everything else is going to hell, at least I've got Cole.

28 STOLEN!

The next morning I'm packing my bag for school when I remember my sketchbook. I left it in the tree house last night. I'd pushed it into the corner when Cole found the article and then got distracted by the kissing.

Man, how could I be so stupid? What if Cole looked at it?

So what? A small voice in the back of my head speaks up. I smile to myself. Would it actually be a big deal if he looked at it? There's nothing incriminating in there.

I mentally scan the pages of my sketchbook and shriek when I remember exactly why it would be a big deal. There's a page dedicated to 'biker boy'. I've drawn his bike, front and centre, with him leaning against a tree in the background, one foot resting on the tree trunk. I drew it not long after he moved in next door. It's one of my best pieces, but there's no way I want Cole knowing I was thinking about him weeks and weeks ago. And drawing him, for goodness sake!

"Everything okay up there?" Mum's voice drifts up from downstairs. She heard the shriek.

"Yeah," I yell back, thinking quickly. "Just a bug."

Besides, I'm panicking over nothing. That particular page is tucked up safely in my bedside drawer. I don't usually rip the pages out of my sketchbook, but that one is special. And I might have wanted to look at it every night before I went to sleep. Sue me.

I grab my bag and sneak out the back door to the tree-house so Mum doesn't start asking questions.

I need my sketchbook. I just do. I don't usually take it to school, except for the odd occasion like when we were doing costume design for the play a few weeks ago and Martha wanted to see what I'd come up with. I showed her and the girls my sketch for Beauty's dress and they agreed it's perfect.

We made a copy to work from and Cassie and I have made it our major project in our textiles class. We're working together, first making the pattern using my design as the starting point, then cutting the pieces from fabric Martha found for us. We're sewing the pieces together now and it should be finished in time for dress rehearsal. And yes, it sucks that it won't be me wearing it, but I feel a sense of achievement knowing that my design has been brought to life. It's going to be stunning.

I'm running late so I'll make an exception today, and take my sketchbook to school with me. Once I get it back in my hands I'm never letting it out of my sight again.

WHEN I GET to the top of the ladder Cole's not there. I'm a little disappointed and I can't tell if he stayed here last night. There wasn't any yelling from next door so maybe he went home after I went inside.

I turn to the corner I pushed my sketchbook into last night. It's empty. My heart stops. Then it restarts, beating a thousand miles an hour as I rush to the corner and start frantically moving things aside.

It's not here.

Breathe. Calm. Deep blue ocean. My Zen goddess mantra isn't helping. My heart is racing, and my hands have gone sweaty. Panic is almost overwhelming me.

Carefully, slowly, I move each of the plastic tubs aside and search under them. Nothing except a dust bunny and what looks like part of a fake fingernail. Weird. I can't remember the last time I wore them, but I guess they're pretty resilient. They'd probably survive a nuclear war. Just like cockroaches. I stifle a hysterical giggle.

Get a grip, Tori.

I open each tub and empty it just to be sure Cole didn't put it away when he was packing up his gear. Nope. Maybe he took it?

Oh, no. He wouldn't.

But it isn't here and that's the only explanation. It's gone. Just gone.

My stomach is churning, and I feel lightheaded. I'm gutted. I cannot believe he would betray me like that. He's asked me about it from time to time and I've let him see the occasional drawing, but he knows how protective I am, and I can't believe he'd go behind my back to look at it. I mean, if he wanted to see it he could have just asked. I'd have let him. Maybe. But to take it? That's next level invasion of privacy.

Although I did leave it here, maybe he took it to keep it safe? Yeah, right. Like some creeper is going to sneak into my treehouse and steal my sketchbook. No, if he was going to touch it he should have put it safely into one of the tubs. Or even brought it to me in the house. Mum would have asked questions but, I dunno, he could have thrown rocks at my window or something. There were a million different options that didn't involve taking it.

I feel like I'm about to cry. I'm frantic, at absolute panic stations and I don't know where to turn next. I think I might even forgive Cole for taking it as long as I get it back safe and sound.

Breathe. I hear Martha's voice in my head and breathe in and out deeply for ten breaths. It doesn't help. I feel slightly less panicky, but anger is building low in my gut. It's like a storm coming. My movements are almost robotic as I climb back down the ladder. I pick up my school bag from the base of the tree and sling it over my shoulder. My fists clench. I start walking. Fast.

I'm almost running by the time I reach Cole's front door, ready for blood. I raise a fist and bang on the door, too far gone in my rage for polite knocks.

It takes too long, and I lift my fist to bang again, just as it opens. Cole's mother opens the door and looks at me without recognition.

"What do you want?" she asks. She glares at me, her tone aggressive. It shakes me out of my rage trance. I take a step back from the door. "I'm looking for Cole."

Her eyes narrow, assessing me. "You're that girl from next door." She huffs and then turns her back and walks away. "Cole! Door!" She yells it up the stairs and then disappears further into the house.

The screen door is still shut and there was no friendly invitation to come inside while I wait. Nope, this is not the cookie cutter romance novel boy next door 'nice Mum'.

She's mean. I feel sorry for Cole before I remember I'm mad at him.

Cole appears a few minutes later. His hair is messy, but he's wearing his school uniform. As he should be, we're already late. Cole's never on time, though. It's the main reason I catch the bus. He rides his motorbike to school and most days he swings into the car park just as the late bell rings.

"Hey." He unlocks the screen door before opening it and stepping out onto the front porch. His eyes are warm, happy to see me. "Was that you banging on the door? What's up?"

For a minute my anger deserts me. The tears threaten again and there's no way I can cry. If I start I might not stop. Nope, it's cry or yell. I pick yell.

Although it comes out more of a wobble than a yell. "I want it back."

He looks confused. "What are you talking about? Are you okay?"

His eyes are intent on my face, concern etched in his expression. He reaches out to pull me into a hug. I resist for a moment but can't help myself. I really need a hug right now. And then the tears start. I'm crying like my heart is broken. Which it is. My life is over without my sketchbook.

"What happened?" He's rubbing my back in small circles and stroking my hair. "You're scaring me, Tori. Talk to me."

Finally, I calm. I feel better now I've got that out of my system. It's stupid. I'm crying over something that's going to be fixed in about two seconds.

"I'm sorry," I say. "I thought I'd lost my sketchbook and then I remembered I left it in the treehouse and when I went to get it, it wasn't there, and then I realised that you probably took it and then I was mad that you looked at it without asking but now I'm just happy that I'm going to get it back."

"Whoa, slow down." His hands are on my shoulders as he watches me with concern. "I did what now?"

"Took my sketchbook. And it's not okay that you looked at it, by the way." I frown up at him and my fists clench at my sides. The anger is still pretty close to the surface despite the tears. I'm all over the place, a mess. "You should have asked first. But you took it and I want it back." My voice is getting louder as I talk, the final sentence almost a yell.

Cole drops his hands from my shoulders and takes half a step back. He looks cagey. "Yeah, I looked at it, you left it there when you went in and I couldn't help myself." He looks at his feet before glancing up from under his thick hair and meeting my eyes with his brilliant green ones. The flecks of gold are not as prominent this morning. "I'm sorry. I should have asked." He looks like he's about to say something else, but I cut him off.

"You should have." I take a deep breath. "Looking at it without my permission is one thing, but taking it is really crossing the line. I want it back."

It's the third time I've said I want it back and he's looking just as confused the first time.

"Tori," he says slowly. "I don't have your sketchbook."

"Don't lie to me, Cole. This isn't something to joke about."

He shakes his head, and there's hurt in his eyes. "You believe I'd take it and then lie to you about it?" He crosses his arms over his chest and his gaze goes hard. "How can you think so little of me?"

"But if you didn't take it than where is it?" I step into

him and jab his chest with my index finger. "Where is it, Cole?"

He catches my hand before I can poke him again. "After you went in last night I stayed a while and looked at your precious sketchbook." He shifts uncomfortably on his feet before he continues. He's hiding something, I'm sure of it. "But then Mum texted and asked me to come home. She had a fight with the jerk and kicked him out. Wanted me to be here in case he tried something."

Well. That explains why his mother was so unfriendly this morning. Or maybe she's always like that. Cole is still speaking.

"I put it back exactly where you left it before I went home."

"You didn't stay there last night?"

He shakes his head. "Nope. Right here, at home.

'Oh."

"Yeah, oh." His voice is cold. "Do you want to apologise now?"

I shake my head right back at him. "Apologise for what?"

We stare at each other for what feels like a lifetime. Then Cole shrugs. "If you have to ask, then you're not the person I thought I knew."

He turns away and pauses with his hand on the screen door like he's waiting for something. But I'm not the one in the wrong here. "You should be apologising to me, Cole."

He turns his back on me and goes into his house. "See you at school."

I'm left standing on his front porch more upset than when I got there. Now I not only lost my sketchbook, I've got a feeling I might have lost Cole too.

29 BACKFLIP

I get to school and I'm even on time. Amazing, really. It feels like a lifetime has passed since I got up this morning.

I walk to my locker, still thinking about the fight with Cole. And it was a fight. Our first fight.

Was I wrong in accusing him?

He was hiding something, at least I thought he was. But maybe I misjudged him. He hasn't lied to me before, and he did try to tell me something before I cut him off. Maybe it was about the thing he was hiding. I feel terrible for not believing him. For automatically thinking he took my sketchbook as soon as I noticed it was missing. I guess that's why he's so upset. I need to apologise to him. Bigtime.

But if he didn't take my sketchbook, then where is it?

I unlock my locker and open it. Or try to. Something is jamming the door shut and I frown. One of my books must have gotten stuck as I closed it yesterday although I don't remember having trouble getting the door shut.

I give it a sharp yank and the world explodes all over

me. I shriek and leap back, my hand going to my chest as my heart rate explodes. It's like the glitter bomb I put in Veronica's locker all those weeks ago, but not glitter. I'm covered in shredded paper.

I step in and pick up a handful hanging off the edge of the door frame and examine it. It's shredded paper, but thicker, like drawing paper instead of the normal sort. It's got stuff written on it. I can make out letters and squiggles on some of the strands. In other places it's just shaded with what looks like charcoal pencil. I would know, it's what I use in my sketchbook.

In fact, the paper's texture is exactly the same as my sketchbook. This is drawing paper.

I bump the door and more paper rains down around me. There's something kind of hard digging into my forehead and I reach up to pull it out of my hair. It's golden and sparkly and a thicker texture than the other paper. My gasp is torn from my throat as I recognise it. It's the cover of my sketchbook.

No. It can't be.

But it is. I know it instinctively. My heart is shrieking in pain.

How did this happen?

I frantically gather the shredded paper from where it's stuck to my body and the door of the locker, then kneel down to collect the pieces from the floor. There's no way it can be, but it is. It's my sketchbook, shredded into a million random pieces of paper.

My eyes get hot and I know I'm about to burst into tears. My heart is breaking. This is my life, and it's been violated. Not only did someone take it, they destroyed it. There's no getting it back. No matter how hard I try to join the pieces into something recognisable, it isn't working. And now that they're wet from the tears flowing unnoticed down my face the paper is going soggy and the charcoal is coming off on my hands.

"Well, well, well." A voice, then movement in my peripheral vision. I ignore it, until a pair of shoes appear right in front of me. Normal school shoes, but the fancy sort. The sort that say 'I'm important'. Veronica's shoes.

I look up to see her smirking down at me and my stomach drops.

She did this. I know it.

She confirms it with her next words.

"How do you like being the one who gets the glitter bomb?" She leans down, almost whispering in my ear. "Do you like it? It's personalised."

There's no fight in me. I'm utterly defeated, kneeling at her feet like a dog. This isn't me.

The surge of hatred brings me to my feet. I glare.

"You... you..." The hate is there but the words aren't. I can't figure out how she got hold of my sketchbook. The words finally come. "I don't know how you did this, but I know why. This is next level sick, Veronica. It's beyond a joke. I didn't destroy anything of yours except your pride."

Veronica smirks. "Maybe. Payback is a bitch, isn't it?"

"That's it. I'm going to the principal." I'm not normally a dobber, but I can't punch her lights out like I want to and something has to be done about this.

"Are you?" Veronica crosses her arms over her chest. She smiles as if she knows something. "You can if you want to. Then I'll have to tell him where I found your precious drawing book." Her smile grows vicious as her hand goes up to her mouth which has formed a perfect 'O' shape. Belatedly I notice one of her red talon fingernails is shorter than the others and I know it's important, but my brain won't give me the reason why.

"Oh, no," she says. "I'll have to tell him what else I found up there."

"What?" My heart plummets to my feet.

"You heard me." She leans in so that only I can hear her. Of course, we've got an audience but I don't see anyone else except her. "You can dob if you like, but if you do? I'll tell everyone where Cole Black spends his nights."

I close my eyes and remember the fake fingernail I found under the plastic tub this morning. It was red. And it hadn't belonged to me after all. Nope. Veronica was in my treehouse.

"You've been watching me?" It comes out as a whisper. Goose bumps creep down my arms.

"Oh, yes. You and your perfect little family and your perfect little boyfriend. Except, his life isn't so perfect, is it? Not when he has to sleep in the neighbour's treehouse."

Cole could get sent into foster care if the authorities investigated, even though he's nearly eighteen. His mother could get into big trouble, and Cole could get moved away to wherever they decide to send him.

This is *bad*. This is even worse than someone finding out for sure that his Mum won Lotto. This could wreck his life. And Veronica has that power.

"Fine, you win," I say. "I won't go to Mr Chapple. I won't say anything to anyone. I hope you're happy."

She smirks and turns to walk away. But she turns back immediately as if she's remembered something. "One more thing," she says, and I brace.

What else?

"I know you're the one who's been sabotaging me." My eyebrows shoot up.

"Play innocent all you like, I know you're behind it." Veronica's hands go to her hips. "It stops, now. Got it?"

I can only nod. She's gone before I can even think of a retort. She's won, not only this round, but the whole freaking game.

30 DISCOVERY

I'm back on my knees gathering my precious, shredded pages when I feel a hand on my shoulder and look up, expecting to see Cole. He's magically appeared every at every other crisis I've had this term.

It's not Cole and disappointment courses through me. Sam stands there, a concerned look on her face.

"Are you okay? What happened?"

I don't expect this from her. She's Cassie's friend, not mine. The only way to tell she cares about anyone is by the degree of meanness in her teasing. She's loud and has no filter. Yet people like her. I guess she's also spontaneous and fun. You get what you see with her and you know exactly where you stand. I've felt like I've been standing on the peripheral, barely tolerated.

Now she frowns. "Isn't that your notebook cover?"

She plucks a strand from my hair and examines it. Yep, more gold sparkles. She's only seen my notebook the one time I took it to rehearsals but she clearly paid attention.

She looks around the small crowd of onlookers, searching. "Where's lover boy? I'd have thought he'd be here for you."

Tears well in my eyes at the mention of Cole. I think I broke things with us this morning. It's one final straw.

I give myself a mental shake. Come on, Tori.

A hand appears in front of my face and I look up at Sam, blinking.

"Get up," she says impatiently. "We've got some butt to kick. Whoever did this to you is going down."

I rub my eyes with the back of my hand, then accept her help, letting her pull me to my feet. I wouldn't have made it otherwise. I was stuck, glued to the floor.

The other students are slowly moving away, thanks to Sam's glare.

She rummages through her backpack and pulls out her lunchbox. She dumps her food into a side pocket of her bag. A sandwich in a ziplock bag and an apple. It's weird what your brain decides to notice when you're in shock. Huh, I guess I'm in shock. I feel a bit foggy and I'm holding the shredded paper close to my body like it's my precious.

Sam starts gathering the pieces from my locker and the door frame, putting them in the lunch box.

"Let me have these," she says. Gently, she takes the shreds I'm hugging and adds them to the container. Then she kneels down to gather what's left on the floor. When everything is in the box she puts the lid on and gives it to me.

"This will have to do for now," she says. "We can work out what to do with it later."

The pages of my beautiful sketchbook are compressed, visible through the clear plastic. The sparkly gold cover glints, interwoven through the rest of the pieces. It's a mess. There's no way we will ever be able to do anything with it.

"Thanks for trying, Sam," I say. "But I think it's a lost cause."

I rummage in my own bag for a handkerchief, so I can blow my nose.

Sam takes my arm and starts pulling me towards the girls' bathroom. She glares at the two girls standing at the sinks, chatting, and they leave quickly. "Wash your face, you'll feel better. Then we can go and kick butt."

I do as she says, letting her hold my book in the box. The water is cool on my hot face and it does make me feel better.

I turn to face her when I'm done.

"The thing is," I say, "I can't kick butt over this. I want to, but I can't."

"What?" Sam's expression is outraged. "It was that Veronica chick, I know it. She's got to pay."

I shake my head, Martha's words loud in my head. "I'm going to have to let Karma sort this one out," I say. "I can't let things escalate any further. It's not worth it."

It's not worth the risk of Cole's secret being let out. Even if he's not talking to me at the moment. Maybe never again, a small voice says. I sigh. Even so, I'll protect him until the day I die.

"Okay, if you say so." Sam doesn't look like she agrees, but she goes along with me. "If you change your mind you let me know."

I nod. "Thanks, Sam. Thanks for helping me."

Sam shrugs and looks away, embarrassed. "I'd do the same for any of my friends," she says. "It's no big deal."

But it is a big deal and we both know it. Last term there's no way we'd have even been happy to be in the same room together, let alone be friends.

I've come a long way since then. And despite my

sadness about my sketchbook there's a small part of me that feels good about how things have changed. I might have lost my crown as the perfect princess and one of the popular ones but being part of the gang of misfits is so much better. I get to be myself and no-one judges me. In fact, they seem to like me for who I am.

Not to start with, obviously. When I first started hanging out with them at lunchtimes they ignored me, mostly. But I gradually started to let my guard down and it seems that the more real I am with them the more they like me. Sam has been the one who I thought would never come around. And I'd convinced myself that I didn't care. But it turns out I do, as evidenced by the warm fuzzies I'm feeling thanks to her calling me a friend just now.

It's clear Martha was right. You do get back what you give. I just wasn't in the right place to discover that until now.

31 SECOND CHANCE

"I heard about what Veronica did."

Things have been strained between Cole and me and this is the first time he's spoken to me since Monday morning. It's now Thursday lunchtime. He's been avoiding me, even going so far as to hang out elsewhere. Someone said he was working on a special project, but I didn't listen. I decided I have to wait for him to make the first move.

Clearly, I was in the wrong, and I'm not sure if he will ever forgive me. All I wanted to do was go crawling to him and beg for forgiveness. To apologise for accusing him, and for even believing that he might have taken my sketchbook in the first place.

But there's a small, stubborn, part of me that's still hurting from the fact that he looked at it without permission. It was private, and he should have asked first.

Not that I'll ever have that problem again. It's gone. I feel like I'm missing a limb. Bereft. All my hopes and dreams were in that sketchbook. It was how I expressed myself, and how I worked out what I was thinking and feeling. It was also a record of my life, more than a diary or journal, and more real than photos could ever be. I'm lost without it.

I look into Cole's emerald green eyes, noticing his long lashes. Why are boys blessed with lashes like that?

"Can we talk?" he asks. "Walk with me, Tori."

I nod, and fall into step beside him, ignoring the stares of our friends. Cassie and Sam both give me subtle thumbs up. I'd told them about what happened with Cole, as much as I could without giving away his secret. But they know we're dating so it was logical that he'd been at my place and I was able to fill them in about how I'd jumped to the wrong conclusion about him taking my sketchbook, and how he'd betrayed my trust by looking at it in the first place. They were sympathetic but didn't have decent advice. Cassie, ever the romantic, told me straight out to forgive him. Sam, the practical one, told me to get over myself and forgive him.

Oh. They did give me advice. It just wasn't advice I was ready to listen to. But after three and a half days without him, and missing him like crazy, I might be ready.

We walk in silence to the perimeter fence behind the Science labs, where we made our escape to the beach all those weeks ago.

"You game?" Cole's eyes are lit up. He's got one hand on the fence post, ready to push it aside so we can squeeze through.

I look guiltily around. There's no-one in sight and lunch time has only just started. We've got heaps of time. I nod, cautiously.

He grabs my bag and throws both his and mine over the fence, just like last time.

Then he pushes on the post and slips through the gap.

He grabs my hand to pull me after him. This time I don't get stuck.

He leans on the fence post to snap it back into place and picks up our bags. My hand is firm in his grip as he tugs me into the bush, towards the path to the beach.

When we burst out of the scrub onto the path there's no-one in sight. Cole continues to hold my hand, interlacing our fingers as we head towards the beach. Once we get to the sand he leads us along the dunes until we find a nice, shady spot under the paperbark trees. Dropping our bags, and my hand, he gestures grandly to the white sand.

"My lady," he says.

I grin and sit beside him, leaning back on my elbows. I take a deep breath of the fresh salt air. "This is nice. Just what I needed, actually."

Cole smiles back. "Nothing like it, is there?"

Then a frown flits across his face and his expression turns serious. "Tori," he says as he turns to face me. "I want to apologise."

My eyes widen. "Oh, no you don't."

"Right," he says, looking down. "You don't want my apology."

It couldn't be further from the truth. I reach out to take his hand, scared he won't let me. He does, but it might as well be driftwood.

"Cole." I wait until he meets my eyes. I was wrong before. I was *in* the wrong before. "You don't have to apologise to me. I have to apologise to you."

His expression lightens, and he squeezes my hand. I rush on before he can say anything.

"What I said to you was wrong. I know you would never do anything to hurt me. I know that. It's just—" My eyes fill with unshed tears and quickly I look away, blinking. I'm not going to burst into tears like some cry baby. I'm not. I take a deep breath and continue. "I was panicking about my sketchbook and I lashed out at you. There's no excuse. I'm ashamed of my actions and I hope you'll forgive me." I look up from under my eyelashes. "Please?"

"Tori, Tori." Cole picks up my other hand so that he's holding both of mine in his large warm ones. "I'll always forgive you."

He leans in and places a gentle kiss on my forehead.

Pulling back, he releases one of my hands, so he can reach behind him to grab his bag. I frown, confused.

"I still owe you an apology." He drops my other hand and starts rummaging around in his bag. Eventually he must find what he was looking for. His movements stop, but he doesn't pull out whatever it is.

"What I did was wrong," he says. I shake my head, but he shushes me. "There's more, Tori. I didn't just look at your sketchbook without permission."

"What?" I'm seriously confused right now. "But you didn't take it. That was Veronica. She saw us, Cole. She was spying on us in the treehouse and she knows you've been sleeping there."

He nods. "I guessed as much. I bet she's threatened to tell everyone, hasn't she?"

"How did you know?"

"You would have rained down a storm on her for what she did. Sam and Cassie would have been right there beside you." He shakes his head. "I was waiting for it. When it didn't happen I realised she must have something over you. The only thing I could think of was me."

I nod, slowly. "I couldn't let her tell your secret. Whether we're dating, or not, she can't do that. Not if it's in my power to stop her."

"I thought as much." He nods. "She doesn't deserve to get away with it. But I understand why you would let her."

"What else did you do?" My mind is still three steps back in the conversation, focused on his comment about 'more'.

He can't hold my gaze. "I shouldn't have done it." Then he looks up and meets my eyes. "But I'm glad I did. Here."

He thrusts something at me. It's bulky and I need both hands to take it from him.

"What is this?"

"Look inside, Tori. Then tell me if I'm forgiven or not."

I do as he says. It's a book, a scrapbook with heavy pages, the kind the serious scrap-bookers use. The cover has a spot for a photograph but it's empty. What's inside takes my breath away.

"Cole!" I look up at him, tears blinding me. "How did you do this? I don't understand."

"Are those happy tears?" he asks cautiously.

I nod. "But how?"

He takes a deep breath, then blows it out. "Thank God," he says softly. Then, louder, he explains.

"I took photos of your sketchbook with my phone. I know I shouldn't have, especially without your permission." He looks at his hands, shaking his head, then back up to meet my eyes. "I'm sorry I overstepped, truly I am."

I nod. "Normally I'd be so pissed off with you right now. But in light of everything that's happened—" I break off and he smiles.

"I was hoping you'd say that."

I make a circular gesture with my hand for him to continue explaining. "Go on."

"After I found out what Veronica had done I thought about what I could do to make you feel better." He points to the book in my hands. "I know it's not the same, but hopefully it helps. I did it at lunchtime and after school this week."

He's printed out the photos of my sketchbook's pages and mounted each shot on a separate page of the scrapbook. It's beautifully done, complete with fancy borders. He photographed every page, thank goodness. It should feel like a supreme invasion of my privacy but I'm just so grateful.

"Thank you, Cole. You don't know how much this means to me."

"I know it's not the same as having the real thing," he says. "But hopefully it will help fill the gap."

"It's perfect," I say. "Absolutely perfect."

32 KARMA

Miss Pretty calls an emergency meeting Saturday morning in the school Hall for the full cast and crew of the production. Dress rehearsal is this afternoon.

We're supposed to show up at midday to get ready for the three p.m. performance. This will be just as if it's the real thing. Full costume and makeup, and music, lights, etc. with a video camera recording everything so we can go over it next week to iron out the bugs.

There's a part of me wishing it's going to be me up on stage. Live performance is a buzz. It's when all the hard work comes together and, if you've done the preparation, it will flow. As the main understudy since Talia pulled out I've been involved more in the rehearsal side of things. I know the lines as well as Veronica but haven't had the practice on stage seeing as it won't be me up there on the night unless a disaster occurs.

No, I'll be in the back with the costume and makeup crew. And I'm strangely okay with that. The C&M'ers feel like family. Yes, once upon a time I would have turned my nose up at them, called them geeks, or losers, or whatever. That was then. Since I've got to know everyone, like, actually know them? They're really cool. They're normal kids, with hopes and dreams, talents and fears, and I'm proud to be able to call them friends.

Cassie and Sam have become really good friends to me, and that's an honour. I'm ashamed of myself when I remember how nasty I was to them both. Thank goodness we've been able to put that behind us. Now it's only mentioned as a way to stir me, usually by Sam. But heaven forbid anyone else try to have a go at me about how I used to be. No, I'm *their* mean girl now.

Only students and teachers are invited to this afternoon's show and not all of them will be there, of course, being the weekend. But we'll have a big enough audience so that it feels authentic and if there are any problems they'll be a bit more forgiving, in theory anyway. Full dress rehearsal is usually a good indication of how Opening Night will go.

For Miss to call us in this early is unusual.

I have a missed call from her, but my phone was flat so I only realised a few minutes ago when I got it off the charger in the kitchen. Her voice message says to call her, but I'll see her in a person at the emergency meeting. Thank goodness she used the group chat to tell everyone to come in for the meeting, otherwise I wouldn't have known about it.

Dad drops me off at school seeing as Mum has taken Jenna to pony club. I had the morning off for once, seeing as it's dress rehearsal day. The play takes priority. Dad's having a rare day at home and tells me to call him when I want him to come and pick me up.

"Sure thing, Dad. Thanks!" I slam his car door and wince. Too hard. "Sorry!"

He shakes his head at me but he's smiling as he drives off.

I go into the hall and find a seat with my friends. Cassie and Sam are already there. Cole slips into the seat beside me just as Miss Pretty walks up onto the stage.

"Hey," he says. He's grinning, his hair all messy.

"You rode?" He nods. I've been forbidden to get on the back of his motor bike, hence the ride from Dad. Until I get my own car I'm stuck relying on my parents. Cole could have got a lift with us, but he likes his freedom too much.

"Alright, attention everyone." Miss Pretty uses her stage voice. She's got a surprising amount of projection for someone her size. Guess she practises what she preaches.

"I've got some bad news," she says. Silence falls. Everyone is paying attention.

"Before I get to that, I want to tell you all how proud I am of you all. You've worked hard, and everything is on track for this afternoon. You're a team and you support each other." She looks around the room and I'm pretty sure she meets the eyes of every person there. I get goose bumps when she gets to me. Whatever she's about to tell us, it's not good.

"In show business nothing is guaranteed. Things happen, and we have to change, adapt. The audience never sees half the drama that happens behind the scenes. What's the first rule of show business?"

"The show must go on?" It's soft and comes from the front, the speaker sounding uncertain.

Miss Pretty nods. "Everybody, what's the first rule of show business?" She raises her hands like a choir conductor and everyone joins together.

"The show must go on!" It's a chorus of voices now. Feet start drumming on the floor and someone starts slow, steady hand clap. It's like one of those TV evangelists, or a rock concert right before the star comes on stage.

Miss Pretty holds one arm high for silence. It's instant. She's got us extremely well trained.

"Today is one of those days. Today is a day that will push our boundaries and test us. Today is a day where we will see what we are made of."

She still hasn't told us the bad news. I'm starting to feel anxious. Is the show cancelled? It can't be, she just said the show must go on.

"I have some bad news, but it's not the end for the show. This is one of the things we prepare for, hoping the preparation won't be needed, but we prepare nevertheless."

Everyone is looking at each other and whispers have started.

"Students!" Miss Pretty calls our attention to the front again.

"What's happened, Miss?" It's Scotty, sitting off to one side.

"Unfortunately I've had some sad news this morning. Veronica Mooney, our leading lady, has been in a car accident."

Gasps from all around the room. More whispers.

"Silence!" Miss Pretty's arm goes up and we hush.

"She's okay, never fear. But she won't be able to perform this afternoon. In fact, she's had to pull out of the production completely."

More gasps, more whispers. Miss Pretty ignores them this time. "This is why we have backup plans," she says. "This is why we have understudies."

Oh. My. God. She means me. I'm the understudy.

An electric shock shoots through me. I feel faint, lightheaded.

This might have been what I thought I wanted, but I don't want it any more. Not even a little bit.

Cole takes my hand and squeezes. "Are you alright?"

I shake my head. "No. I'm not. Cole, I don't want this!"

My heart is slamming in my chest and my eyes are wild, darting everywhere. The room is in turmoil as people look around. They're looking for the understudy. They're looking for me.

"And while we're sorry for what happened to Veronica, the show must go on." Miss Pretty raises her volume to carry over the crowd. "Tori Pearson, can you come up here, please?"

"Hey, look at me." Cole brings my focus back to him. "You've got this, okay? It's what you wanted."

"I don't want it anymore," I say. "I'm quite happy to sit backstage with my C&M peeps."

Cole grins. "Yeah, yeah. I know. But that's scaredy-cat Tori talking. Right now, we need the tiger."

I blink. "The tiger?"

His grin grows. "The tiger."

He squeezes my hand and leans in close, kissing my cheek. "You've got this, Tori. I believe in you." He takes my other hand as well. "You've got to believe in yourself."

Around us the noise is escalating. Feet are drumming on the floor again. Scotty's voice comes loud and clear. He's up on stage with Miss Pretty.

"Tori!" Clap, clap, clap.

"Tori!" Clap, clap, clap.

Other students join in. Soon, the whole hall full of kids is chanting my name.

Cole squeezes my hands again. "You've got this."

He stands and pulls me to my feet and into the aisle. Cassie and Sam are giving me encouraging looks.

"Get up there, girlfriend!" says Sam.

"You've got this," says Cassie.

"Go on," says Cole. "We'll be here."

I nod, and then it hits me. I'm going to be Beauty. I feel the joy flow from deep inside. I'm going to be Beauty! It's bubbling over now and I grin, big.

I'm sorry for what happened to Veronica, I truly am. But Karma kicked her butt. And now it's my time to shine. Which is cheesy, but also true.

I look around the hall. All eyes are on me. Scotty whoops from the stage and the chant gets louder.

I take off at a run and sprint to the stage, bounding up the stairs. Scotty grabs my hand and raises it high. Miss Pretty takes my other hand and does the same.

"I did try to ring you earlier," Miss Pretty says quietly. "I wanted to give you a heads up. But now you know."

"Yep," I say. "It's all good."

And it is. It's perfect.

33 QUEEN VEE

Miss Pretty tells me that Veronica both broke her legs in the car crash. She's in a bad way, and her Mum, who was driving, is in a coma. They're lucky to be alive.

She doesn't tell me this lightly. I think she knows I'm freaking out and am hoping that it's a temporary setback. No such luck.

"I thought you'd be happier about this, Tori," says Miss Pretty.

"So did I," I say. I take a deep breath. "Don't worry Miss, I won't let you down. I know my lines and Scotty will help me with the blocking. Everyone will."

Miss Pretty nods. "It's a lot of pressure, but we'll all be there to help you to pull it off. The audience won't know any better."

I'm about to walk away when Miss calls me back. "Tori?"

I turn.

"About that audition scene?"

I nod. I know where this is going. "I know, Miss. I over-played it. I saw how Veronica did it and I know I can do the same."

Miss Pretty smiles. "That's good, but I want you to be yourself up there. Your audition scene was over the top, yes. But don't sell yourself short. You don't have to be a Veronica clone."

That stuns me. She's right, not just about the play either. I sometimes wonder how aware the teachers are about the social politics of the school. Some are more aware than others, clearly. And Miss Pretty might be the most aware of them all.

BACKSTAGE IN THE COSTUME ROOM, Cassie and Sam are helping me to try on the outfits. Veronica and I are very similar in size, fortunately. She has more in the chest department though, so we're having to improvise with padded bra's and fake cleavage.

There's a commotion at the door and then Tiffany and Josephine walk in, followed by several of the other girls I used to call my friends. I was never really the leader, except in my own head. I smile to myself, remembering when that had seemed so important. To be honest, I wasn't a very good friend to them. It's no wonder they switched to Veronica so easily.

"Vee!" Josephine is at my shoulder, talking loudly. "This is so great! You're going to be amazing."

At first, I don't register that it's me she's talking to. I don't think of myself as 'Vee' any more.

"Vee!" Tiffany echoes. "This is so great!"

"This is like, awesome." Josephine again. "Come on, we're getting milkshakes to celebrate."

"What?" I don't believe what I'm hearing.

"Yeah, we've missed you, Vee." Tiffany bumps my shoulder with hers as though we're best buddies. Behind her I see Sam rolling her eyes and I try not to laugh.

Trent shoulders his way through the crowd. "Come on, Vee." He grabs my hand and starts pulling me out of the room. "We're out of here. Later, losers!"

I dig my heels in and try to pull out of his grasp, but he's got a firm grip and isn't letting go.

What on earth is happening? I look back over my shoulder at the girls but they're no help. Sam is bent over double, laughing herself silly, while Cassie just shrugs. "Later," she mouths.

"Yeah, like, later, losers," says Tiffany.

"Later, losers," echoes Josephine.

Trent still has my hand and is towing me along and the girl posse closes in around me. Even if I broke free of Trent I'd still be stuck so I give in and go with the flow. I'll sort this mess out when we get outside.

We weave our way through the backstage corridors and are nearly outside when we run into Cole. He's got his head down and his hands in his pockets, deep in thought. Heading towards costumes where he no doubt thinks he'll find me.

"Out of the way, loser." Trent purposely shoulders Cole aside, dropping his grip on my hand to do it.

I stop, dismayed. "Trent!"

Coles head snaps up at my voice. He takes in the group I'm with, eyeing Josephine and Tiffany like they're bugs beneath his shoe. Which they totally are. His eyes move to me and I shake my head at him, trying to convey everything that just happened with one look.

Trent picks that moment to put his arm around me and start moving us forward again.

"Let's blow this joint," he says. No doubt he thinks he's cool. I can't believe I ever wanted to go out with him.

I try to fight his arm off from around me but he's not letting go. He has momentum and a pack of girls helping him to move us forward, away from Cole and my friends. My real friends.

I look back and see Cole, still standing to the side of the hallway, his mouth in a grim line. His eyes meet mine and this time it's him who shakes his head. He looks gutted as he turns his back on me and walks away.

I start fighting Trent for real but by the time I break free it's too late. Cole has disappeared.

"WHAT'S WRONG WITH YOU?" I put my hands on my hips and glare at Trent. I include Josephine and Tiffany for good measure.

"Milkshakes, Vee," says Trent. "Get with the program."

"I'm not going for milkshakes with you."

"You can have something else," says Tiffany. "Jeez, what's your problem?"

"My problem?" I sputter. "My problem? Where do I even start. Oh, I know. We're not friends anymore!"

We never really were, not that I knew it back then. But now I do know how real friends act. These girls, and Trent, are not my friends.

"Vee...," says Josephine, her tone of voice suggesting I'm being unreasonable.

"And that's another thing. My name is not Vee. It's Victoria."

Josephine huffs. "Fine, Tori."

"No." I scowl. "Only my friends get to call me Tori."

"Well. If that's how you feel you can go back and join the losers," Tiffany says. She folds her arms across her chest and sneers at me. "We're no longer friends."

"Before you go calling other people losers, you should take a good, hard look at yourselves. You call yourselves friends?" I'm in full rant now. There's no stopping me. "Friends care about each other. Like, for example, if your friend is in hospital you might go and visit her. Or if your other friend suddenly got told she had to take on the leading role in the play you might realise she needs a minute to get ready. You know, friendship. Thinking about what another person needs and doing that, even if it doesn't fit in with your plans to go and drink milkshakes."

"Whatever." Tiffany and Josephine say it at the exact same time. Then they turn on their heels together, and march right up the corridor and outside. The other girls follow them, leaving Trent.

Trent, at least, looks ashamed of himself. "Sorry, Victoria," he says. "I wasn't thinking. Guess I got caught up in the moment."

"That's okay," I say. "But you do realise I have a boyfriend, don't you?"

His eyes widen. "You do?"

"You should try paying attention to other people every once in a while," I say. "Later, Trent."

I turn and walk away, leaving him standing there.

I realise I have an audience. Cassie and Sam are at the bend in the corridor and I'm betting they heard everything. This is confirmed as I get closer to them.

Sam is beaming. She holds her palm up for a high five. "That was awesome," she says. "You really told them."

"You're my hero," says Cassie. She steps forward and hugs me. "And I'm really proud to be able to call you my friend."

My heart swells with gratitude at her words. I smile. "Thanks. Me too."

"There's just one little thing." Sam is frowning. "Cole didn't stick around to hear your little speech. He took off right after Trent called him a loser. I dunno, I thought he had thicker skin than that."

"It wasn't what Trent said," says Cassie. "It's what he saw. Think about it from his point of view. Tori just got the lead role and all of a sudden she's back to being Queen Vee."

Far out. That's just what I was afraid of.

"I've got to go. I've got to find him and explain."

Cassie nods. "Just be back here by two so we can get your hair and makeup done."

I look at my watch. It's already eleven. I don't have a lot of time.

34 GOOD PERSON

I ring Dad to come and get me. He's there within ten minutes, thank goodness. I have a sneaking suspicion I know where to find Cole. The treehouse is the first place I'll look. If he's not there, honestly, I don't know where else to try.

But there's something else I need to do first, before I go and find Cole. I've got to visit Veronica.

"Can we make a detour to the hospital, Dad?"

"Sure, sweetheart. What's going on?" Dad flicks me a concerned look before returning his attention to the road.

I explain about how one of the actors in the play was in a car accident and broke her legs, right before dress rehearsal. Maybe I should mention it's Veronica? Dad's attention is on the road and a driver up ahead who jammed on the brakes for no apparent reason, so I let him concentrate.

I'm not sure why I want to visit her. My gut is telling me it's the right thing to do and I was acting on instinct when I asked Dad to swing past the hospital. I think on it as we travel.

No, it's not to rub it in that Karma bit her backside. Although that's tempting. It's just that it would suck if it happened to me and all of my *friends* decided to go for milkshakes instead of coming to visit.

She's got no-one. Her Dad is in jail as far as I know, and her Mum is in a coma. I can't begin to imagine what she's going through but I want to offer my support. It's the least I can do.

We arrive at the hospital and I find out which room she's in at the front desk.

"Do you want me to come with you?" Dad asks.

"No, that's okay." I shrug. "Unless you want to? She's in Ward B."

I know they've got history, or I'm assuming as much from my Google search on Veronica and her father. I definitely should have mentioned to my Dad that it's her that I'm here to see. I open my mouth to tell him but he's already walking away.

"I'll just grab a quick coffee," he says over his shoulder.

I FIND Veronica's ward and check at the nurses' station which room she's in. She's got a room to herself down the end of the corridor, complete with a window.

The hospital seems to have an open-door policy. None of the rooms have closed doors, and most of them seem to have multiple beds separated by curtains. Veronica is lucky to have her own room. I knock on the open door and call "Hello?" before I walk in.

Veronica is watching the door and her face screws up as she sees me. She's lying there, both legs wrapped in plaster and supported by a rope and pulley system hanging off a frame attached to the bed. There's a drip in her arm, some kind of clear fluid pumping into her vein. A television is mounted on the wall with picture but no sound. The room is nice, it has an ensuite toilet and shower, but it's got to be hard to be stuck here.

"Hey," I say, approaching the bed.

"Come to gloat?" The words are scathing, but there's no feeling behind them. "I don't care, just say what you have to say and then leave me alone."

I swallow. "I just came to see how you are."

She gives me a hard look. Whatever she sees in my face must satisfy her because the tension leaves her shoulders. "Fine. I'm fine."

"Okay then." This is awkward. "Veronica, I know we haven't been the best of friends—"

She snorts. "We're not friends, Victoria. Don't kid yourself. The only reason I went to that school was to take you down."

"What? Why?" It's the moment of truth. "What have I ever done to you?"

"It wasn't you, Tori." The voice comes from behind me. "It was me."

My dad walks into the room and approaches the bed. "Hi, Veronica."

"Coach." Veronica spits the words. "I trusted you. My family and I, we welcomed you into our home and you betrayed us. My dad's in jail because of you."

My father stands with his shoulders slumped like he's carrying the weight of the world on his back. He looks Veronica right in the eyes. "I'm so very, very sorry you got caught up in it. Neither your father or I wanted you to be involved."

"I am involved. Mum and I had to leave town. We had

to change our last name, and I haven't seen Dad for three months. And now Mum's in a coma." Her chest hitches and I can tell she's trying not to lose it. I move to her bedside table and pour a glass of water from the plastic pitcher. Wordlessly, I hand it to her, creating a barrier between her and my father while she composes herself.

She takes a sip of water and hands the glass back, taking a deep, shaky breath. I move aside so Dad can see her again, trusting him to make things right.

"I can't tell you much," he says. "Just know that there's a plan. I'm one of the good guys, so is your Dad. But we had to play it like we did so that your mother and you didn't get caught up in the cross-fire. It should all be resolved soon and your Dad will be back with you before you know it."

"Did you not hear the part where Mum's in a coma?" Veronica isn't backing down. It's a good thing there isn't a heart monitor attached to her, the nurses would have been in here by now.

"That does complicate things," says Dad. "What do you remember about the accident?"

"It was stupid. We were driving into town, doing a late-night ice-cream run, and singing along to the radio. A dog ran out in front of the car and when Mum swerved to miss it she hit a telegraph pole." She huffs out a fake laugh. "The dog ran off, not a scratch. The telegraph pole was fine too. But the car flipped. Mum hit her head on the windscreen and hasn't woken up. It was lucky I could reach my phone to call emergency."

I wince. Dad closes his eyes momentarily and then takes a step closer.

"I'm here for you, Veronica. As long as you need help. Your Mum too, when she wakes up."

Veronica promptly bursts into tears. It's the last thing I

expect. Dad steps in and awkwardly pats her shoulder. She throws her arms around his waist and buries her head in his stomach.

My Dad's fit, but he has a bit of a beer belly. And while it's weird that Veronica is touching him, it's exactly what I would have done if it had been me lying in that hospital bed. I guess they really were close.

Dad's awkward shoulder pat morphs into an awkward back pat which seems to last forever. Eventually, Veronica's sobs subside, and she pulls back. Wordlessly, I hand her the box of tissues from the bedside table.

"You okay?" Dad's voice is gruff.

Veronica smiles. It's wobbly, but it's there. "I will be," she says. "Thank you."

We don't stay long after that. When the nurses come in to do their rounds we say our goodbyes.

"I'll come and visit you tomorrow, if you like." I smile as warmly as I can. This is all way too weird, but I get the feeling that Veronica is a part of my life now. "I'll bring my Mum, too." I look at Dad. "Does she know about all this?"

Dad shakes his head. "She knew I was doing under-cover work, but she doesn't know the details. I'm not allowed to talk about it."

"Oh." I don't know what to make of that. Why would he step in to help Veronica and her mother now? He clearly feels bad about what happened to them, though. "I'll just tell her you're a friend from school. She'll make sure you're being looked after properly and that things are happening with your mother. Tests or whatever. She's good at stuff like that."

Veronica nods. "Thanks. I'd like that."

∽

DAD IS silent on the way home. All he'll say is that it's part of an ongoing investigation. I keep pushing. I need to understand what happened, why Veronica hated me.

"It's unlucky that Veronica got caught up in it," Dad says eventually. I've worn him down. "Her father's a good man. Our task force had to take down the operation from the inside and I was able to form a bond with Veronica's father. I used Veronica and my position as her soccer coach to do it. I'm not proud of it, but it was the only way. Once her father realised he could trust me he worked with us."

"But why did he get arrested?" That's the bit that's puzzling me. "Why did he go to jail?"

"These are dangerous men, Tori. The only way to protect Veronica and her family was to make it look as if he wasn't working with us. So he's in protective custody until we make the arrests higher up the food chain. It's complicated, but it will all be sorted out soon."

He pulls into our driveway and stops the car. "Tori," he says. His face is grim. "You can't repeat any of what I've just told you. Not a word."

"I understand, Dad." And I do. But surely Cole doesn't count.

"And if Veronica was as mean to you as I suspect she might have been, you're going to have to come up with a really good story about why you're suddenly friends."

"Don't worry about that," I say. "The whole reason I went to visit her in the first place was because her supposed *real friends* decided to go out for milkshakes instead of going to the hospital. Even though we don't get on, I couldn't let her go through something like that on her own. No matter if she hates me."

"You're a good person, Tori," says Dad.

I only hope that Cole thinks so too.

35 TREASURE

I'm starting to feel pressure now. The hospital visit took way, way longer than I'd hoped. Good outcome, but still. It's half past one and I still need to find Cole.

I only hope he's in the treehouse.

I dash upstairs to my room before I go out the back. There's something I need to get, and it's important.

As I climb the ladder I find it hard to grip the rungs, my hands are shaking so badly. My head pops up through the gap in the floorboards. The sun is at the same angle it was the first time I found Cole up here and he's backlit, the full halo effect in action. I'm so relieved that he's here.

"Hey," I say. I haul myself the rest of the way into the treehouse and sit on the edge, my legs dangling. I put the plastic folder on the floorboards beside me, well away from the drop.

"Can you not do that?" He sounds worn out, tired, but I can't see his expression due to the sun in my eyes. "I don't want you to fall to your death. What would all your *friends* do without their Queen Vee."

"It's like that, is it?" I climb all the way into the treehouse and pull one of the plastic tubs so that it blocks the hole. "Happy?"

"No, I'm not happy." He moves to the side, further away from me. "Why are you here, Tori?"

"Last time I checked this was my treehouse, Cole." I draw his name out. "Why are you here?"

He snorts. There's shouting from next door and I grimace. "Oh."

"Yeah, oh. I'm having a shit day. First my girlfriend decides to ditch me in favour of her loser friends who think everyone else is a loser. Then I get home to find my mother's dropkick boyfriend is back, and when I offer to kick him out she tells me to stop interfering."

"Cole..." I feel so much for him in that moment.

"Don't, Tori. I don't want your pity."

I feel so much, and none of it's pity.

"Listen here, buddy. And you listen good! In fact, if you'd hung around for just a minute longer at school you'd know this already, but that's okay, I don't mind repeating myself."

"What are you talking about?" I can see Cole's expression and he's got that cold look in his eyes. But I know it's a mask. It's his way of protecting himself.

"You know what, I can't actually remember what I said. Cassie and Sam can give you the blow by blow. Hell, Sam probably caught it all on her phone. Bottom line, I told those losers, my ex *friends*, where to go. I told them I don't need friends like them, and that they need to take a good hard look at themselves." I shake my head. "They were going for milkshakes, Cole. Can you believe it? Veronica's in hospital with two broken legs and they're going for milkshakes. They expected me to pick up right where I was before. It's like they don't know how to function without someone to follow around."

"Did you say two broken legs?"

"Oh, you didn't know?"

Cole shakes his head.

"Yeah, she said her mother swerved to miss a dog and ran off the road. Her Mum's in a coma, Cole. She's got no-one. And her so called friends are off having milk shakes!"

"She said?"

"I've just been to see her."

"Right."

I realise how it must sound. I prioritised Veronica over Cole. "She's got no-one. And it turns out my dad knows her from before, and is friends with her dad and the jail time is all some sort of plan so the bad guys don't find out he was working to take them down. So that explains why she was out to get me. She thought my Dad turned on her family when she trusted him and wanted to hurt me as payback. But it's all cleared up now."

"Well that's good then. I'm glad that all worked out." His voice is heavy with sarcasm. "And now you can hook up with Trent and everything will be perfect."

I'm stunned.

For a minute I don't have words. We sit in silence, our eyes locked. His fists flex. So do mine. Finally I speak. "Is that what you really think?"

If it is, then I'm done.

"I don't know what to think. You tell me, Tori. 'Cos from where I'm sitting I'm the one making all the effort. And as soon as you got what you wanted, as soon as you got your lead part, you ditched me. You waltzed out of school to go and get milkshakes with Trent."

"I didn't go and get milkshakes with Trent. Haven't you been listening? I went to the hospital to visit Veronica!"

"I've been sitting here this whole time thinking you were with that jerkwad. I thought you'd dumped me, Tori. Without even giving me the courtesy of telling me. I thought I'd lost the best thing that ever happened to me."

"I'd never do that!" Tears flow hot down my cheeks, but I ignore them. His words sink in and I find myself repeating them back to him. How can I not? They're true for me too. "You're the best thing that ever happened to me, Cole. And my life isn't perfect, not by a long shot. But not quite perfect is exactly the way I like it."

I wipe at my face with the back of my hand.

He's staring, eyes wide. "Tori..." he begins.

"No, Cole. Don't. I can't do this now. I've got to get back to school." Right on cue my phone chimes with a text. It's Cassie.

Where are you?

I quickly text back. On my way!

It's two o'clock and I've got sixty minutes before the curtain opens.

I look up from my phone to find Cole is right there.

"Tori, Tori, Tori," he says. Then his arms wrap around me and he's kissing me.

I lose myself in his kiss. It makes everything alright. I'm safe here, wrapped in his arms and the world is a better place. Then his tongue touches mine and the world explodes. Fireworks in my stomach, dancing around my brain, and my head is lost to the feeling. I pull Cole even tighter. I never want to be parted from him, not ever again.

Eventually, forever and yet no time at all, he pulls back. He kisses the corners of my mouth, like he did the first time, then rests his forehead on mine. We're both out of breath.

"Wow," I say, softly.

"Wow," He repeats. That was some kiss.

My phone chimes again.

I hold it out and we read it together. It's Cassie.

Hurry!

"Do you need a ride?"

I nod. "I do." Sure, my Mum has forbidden me from hopping on the back of Cole's bike. But desperate times call for desperate measures. It's only the dress rehearsal, but it still counts as an emergency. I'm counting it, anyway.

Cole's moved the plastic tub back to where it came from and has one foot on the ladder when I remember the treasure I collected from my bedside drawer before I came up here. I put my hand on his arm. "Wait."

He turns back, a puzzled frown on his face.

"I have something for you."

I retrieve the plastic folder from the corner where it landed. Ironically, it's the same corner my sketchbook was last seen. "This is for you."

Cole opens the folder slowly. He licks his lips, nervous. Then his eyes widen. "This is amazing!"

I've given him the one sketch I've saved from my sketchbook. The one of him and his bike.

"I can't keep this." He tries to hand it back to me. "This is from your sketchbook. It's the only page left in existence."

"I want you to have it," I say. "I've got my beautiful memories in the scrapbook you put together for me. That's all I need. I'll do more drawings when I'm ready. This one is for you."

"Thank you," he says. He brushes a gentle kiss on my forehead. "I'll treasure it always."

A week later and it's opening night. We've got an hour until the curtains open. I've just arrived backstage and am walking into the costume and makeup room, Cole by my side. He's supposed to be up in the scaffolding already, manning the lights.

He's going to be late.

He draws me close and finds my lips with his. Our kiss starts slow and decadent and builds. His arms tighten around me as our tongues dance. The butterflies are exploding, and I forget where I am.

"Tori, get over here!" Cassie is standing beside the main makeup chair, tapping her foot. "I'm on a deadline. You can kiss the boy later."

I pull back from Cole and laugh. "It's all good. If you could make me look decent in ten minutes last week, imagine what you can do in a whole hour!"

The full dress rehearsal had gone off. Not without a hitch. Definitely not perfect. But we got through it and the audience was brilliant.

I've spent all this week rehearsing madly. Scotty has

been a huge help, and Cole has been there supporting me every step of the way. He's hardly left my side.

"You good?" Cole asks.

I nod. "You?"

"Never better." He grins, his eyes sparkling.

The day of the full dress rehearsal his mother had kicked her boyfriend out for good. After the yelling was out of the way they'd had a deep and meaningful discussion and decided to part ways. That's what she'd told Cole, anyway. And he hasn't been back so it's all good.

Trent, Josephine and Tiffany have faded into the background and to be honest I haven't given them a second thought.

"First things first," says Sam. She grins. "We've got something for you, O leading lady."

She's been a bit down lately so it's good to see her smiling.

We'd had a conversation about it a few days ago.

"What's up?" I'd asked. She gave me a look, an eyebrow arched.

"You're not your usual bouncy self. I notice these things." I put my hands on my hips. "So spill."

A few months ago, I wouldn't have noticed, and even if I did I wouldn't have cared. Funny what a difference a change in perspective can make.

"She broke up with Travis," said Cassie, and Sam frowns at her.

"I thought you two were golden."

"Yeah, I guess," said Sam. "But there's got to be more, you know? We got on well but there was no spark. Really, we were just friends who dated."

"Does Travis think that too?"

"He agreed to be friends, if that's what you mean." She shrugs. "Not sure if he meant it, but time will tell, I guess."

Even though it was mutual, and Sam's idea in fact, she's been down in the dumps. But not right now. Her mischievous grin lights up her whole face.

"Alright, let me have it." I'm expecting a practical joke of some kind. A pair of crutches in case I break a leg, or some fake boobs to help in the cleavage department.

Instead I get some of the most thoughtful gifts I've ever received.

Cassie has made me cupcakes, her specialty, and she's decorated them with characters from the play. "Ooooh, thank you," I say. "They're gorgeous. Chocolate?"

"Of course." Cassie grins. "Do you like the Beast?"

I nod. "I do."

The Beast is a silhouette, outlined in piped icing. Half his face is beast-like, the other half is human. "Nicely done."

Sam has given me a box of Ferraro Rocher chocolates. "How did you know they're my favourites?"

She shrugs. "You let it slip one day in class. I just remembered."

Cole has something for me too.

"I've actually got two things," he says. "I enlisted my partners in crime for this."

He takes something Cassie is holding out to him and passes it to me. "I hope you like it."

He seems almost shy.

I look closely at the item. It's not wrapped, but it doesn't need to be. It's a sketchbook. The cover is purple with bold splashes of colour. I throw my arms around his neck for a quick hug. "It's perfect."

"The other thing is more of an activity, and it won't kick

in until the summer holidays." He grins. "I was going to tell you later, but now is as good a time as any."

"The suspense is killing me," I say. "Spit it out."

"You know how you love the beach, but your Mum won't let you surf?"

I nod.

"Well, the surf club is looking for volunteer surf life-savers over the holidays. I put our names down." He gestures to Cassie and Sam. "The girls are doing it too."

Cassie and Sam both nod, huge smiles on their faces. "I'll miss a few weeks while I'm in France, but Sam will be there the whole time," says Cassie.

Cole's grin is huge. "You'll have to do Surf Life Savers every weekend, so you know what you're doing when you're on patrol. They have competitions and stuff. It's loads of fun."

"I'm not sure Mum will agree to this," I say.

"She already has," says Cole. "I talked to her a few days ago. It's for a good cause, giving back to our community, and she loved the idea."

"She agreed? That surprises me." It surprises me even more that Cole has talked to her about it.

"And the best part is, seeing as we'll be at the beach already, I'll be able to teach you to surf."

My smile threatens to break my face in two. "This is so awesome!"

We have to rush to get ready after that. The girls help me with my costume and makeup. The other cast members are there with the rest of the costume and makeup crew helping them get ready. Any nerves I have are chased away by the party-like atmosphere.

Before I know it, it's time to take our places for the opening scene.

Mum, Dad and Jenna are in the audience tonight, front and centre. Veronica is with them. They picked her up from hospital on a day pass. She'll be sitting in the aisle in one of those weird wheelchairs with both her legs sticking out in front of her. I don't know how she doesn't overbalance. Maybe the handles are weighted.

Her mother finally woke up a few days ago and she's going to be okay. They're keeping both of them in hospital though. Thank goodness. My newfound 'friendship' with Veronica probably wouldn't stretch so far as sharing a bedroom with her, or even my house.

THE SHOW GOES WITHOUT A HITCH. Nothing the audience would notice, anyway. Minor hiccups are normal, as is the occasional missed cue. That's what the coach at the side of the stage is for.

It's a huge success and we get a standing ovation.

Miss Pretty and Martha join the cast and crew for the final curtain call and we all take our bows to the audience. It's such a buzz. I love it.

The truth is, I would have been happy staying behind the scenes. But I'm glad I was able to step up and help out when needed. I'm not proud of the way I've behaved towards Veronica. Even knowing why she was a biatch to me, what I did to her was immature and mean. My reasons seem so petty and spiteful now I look back at it. I'm ashamed of myself.

I'm going to be a better person.

I'm not aiming for perfect, just better.

MUM COMES BACKSTAGE AFTERWARDS, while I'm getting changed out of the final costume.

"Tori, you were excellent!" She hugs me. "Did you have fun?

"The best," I say. "It was awesome."

"What was your favourite part?" Mum asks.

"You know, just being part of something bigger than myself. I love that I helped create this experience for everybody."

Mum smiles. "That's great, honey. It doesn't matter if you're the star of the show or one of the makeup girls. Everyone has a part to play. It's the teamwork that can make or break a show like this."

"So you honestly wouldn't have cared if I was just one of the makeup girls?" I'm pushing my luck a bit, but I can't help it.

Mum shakes her head. "Of course not. Just as long as you're involved. It's a great experience."

"Seriously? I thought you had your heart set on me playing the lead role."

"You don't have to be perfect all the time."

That's news to me. But maybe I've misinterpreted Mum's demands for perfection. Maybe she wasn't wanting that for me at all. The conversation at family dinner that night I admitted I hadn't won the leading role comes back to me. 'Perfect is good, but only as long as you're happy', she'd said. I hadn't really believed her at the time.

"Are you sure about that, Mum?" I ask. "I thought 'perfect' was what you expected of me."

"No, Tori," she says. "Perfection is overrated. As long as you get in and have a go at a lot of different things then I've done my job as your parent. You might not excel at everything, but you won't know if you enjoy it until you try. And a lot of the time the only way to get good at something is to practise."

"Oh," I say. "That explains a lot about my childhood."

Mum smiles but lets the subject drop.

And me? I've learnt a valuable lesson.

Perfection is overrated.

Not quite perfect all the way.

EPILOGUE

Four weeks later

I'm standing at my window, hairbrush in my hand, trying to get the tangled mess under control.

I have no shame. I'm watching Cole.

He's in the driveway with his head under the bonnet of a car. I've got no idea what sort of a car it is, but it's bright and shiny and new. It belongs to his mother's new boyfriend.

That boyfriend is standing right beside Cole, pointing to something on the engine. At least, I think that's what he's doing. I could be wrong. They might just be leaning over the engine to strengthen their lower backs for all I know.

It doesn't matter. The point is, Cole's mother has a new boyfriend and he's the sort of man who, one, drives a nice shiny, brand new car, and two, is happy to spend time with Cole looking under the bonnet.

Cole deserves to have a good man in his life and it looks like his mother has finally found him one.

I finish brushing my hair and throw it up into a messy bun.

I've graduated from the high pony tail, and there's no way I'm straightening my hair any more. I shudder. Been there, done that, not ever going back. #NeverEver. I've come a long way since those days. Listen to me, it was only eight or nine weeks ago. But it feels like forever. Cole says I'm a lot more relaxed than I used to be, and he likes me *being me*. So do I.

My new sketchbook sits on my dresser. It's not so new anymore. It's more than half full and it's nearly time start looking for a new one. I'm drawing a lot more nowadays, that's for sure.

I watch Cole as he stands and wipes his hands on an old towel. He's laidback and casual in his board shorts and tee. The boyfriend holds out his hand and Cole shakes it, grinning, before holding his fist out for a fist bump. I smile to myself as Cole walks to the front of my house and disappears.

Moment later I hear a knock on the door, then Mum's voice.

'Tori! Cole's here!"

I take one last look in the mirror.

I'm wearing cute denim cutoff shorts over my swimmers.

We're heading for the beach today, and when we get there Cole is giving me a surf lesson. It's not even tacked onto Surf Lifesaving. Mum has given her blessing for me to learn to surf, as long as it's Cole teaching me.

Go figure. Cole was on the top of her list— 'boys to keep away from my daughter'— and now he's her favourite. I guess she got to know him over this last term of school, and she judged him on his actions, not his reputation.

I fly down the stairs and straight into Cole's arms. He takes a step back from the impact and his breath leaves him with an oomph.

Whoops.

"Hey," he says., recovering.

"Hey, yourself."

His arms wrap me tight and he kisses me.

His kiss feels like home. I spend every spare moment with Cole and it's not enough. This boy completes me, and as long as we're together I know, things might not be perfect, but they're exactly the way they're meant to be.

We've got our own sort of perfection going on.

And I love it.

FINAL WORDS

Did you enjoy this book? If so, please (pretty please) leave a review and share with your friends!

Book Three, Sam's story *More Than #This*, is being released in August 2019.

If you'd like an exclusive email when it's available you can sign up using the link below.

Go to —>>

https://geni.us/TessMackayMoreThanThis

Book one in the *Sweet #Challenge High* YA Romance series, **Just Say #Yes**, is out now.

Available to buy on Amazon**,** or read it FREE on Kindle Unlimited.

Go to —>> **https://geni.us/JustSayYes**

ALSO BY TESS MACKAY

A Sweet #Challenge High YA Romance series

Book 1 - Just Say #Yes

Go to —>> https://geni.us/JustSayYes

Book 2 - Not Quite #Perfect

Go to — >>https://geni.us/NotQuitePerfect

Book 3 - More Than #This (coming August 2019)

Let Me Know Link —>> https://www.
subscribepage.com/tessmackaybooks_morethanthis

Each book in the series is a Stand Alone Sweet YA Romance set in Australia

Want to be included in my Newsletter mailing list?

Go to —>>

https://geni.us/TessMackayNewsletter

ACKNOWLEDGMENTS

I can't believe it's finally here. My second young adult book, done and dusted! What did you think of Tori's story? I knew there was more to her when she was being a biatch to Cassie in Just Say #Yes and I had to explore it. I had a lot of fun with her and Cole.

I have a few thank you's.

My family is awesome and they don't seem to mind when I disappear into the creative zone for hours at a time. Love you guys xx.

My fellow writers, who I catch up with online and occasionally in real life, are so supportive and I have to say, this indie writing community is the best!

And last but not least, to anyone who has taken the time to read this book - thank you x.

If you could take a few minutes to leave a review I'll be forever grateful.

You can find me online at my website www.tessmackaybooks.com. And I love Instagram #naturally.

Until next time, Happy reading,

Tess x

ALL ABOUT TESS

Romantic. Loves YA. Searching for the ultimate book boyfriend, one book at a time.

Tess Mackay lives by the beach in country Australia. She loves all things creative and can usually be found with her iPhone in hand checking out the latest thing on social media.

facebook.com/TessMackayBooks

twitter.com/TessMackayBooks

instagram.com/TessMackay

GLOSSARY

Some of the Australian terms used in this book

Dinking – Doubling on a pushbike, usually the second person sits on the handlebars, or sometimes on the back if there's a parcel rack.

Ditch – As in ditch school. To leave early without permission. To wag.

Dobber – Someone who tells on you. Usually the authorities, or an authority figure, but sometimes your siblings or other friends. Being a dobber is generally accepted as being the lowest of the low.

Surf Life Saving – Beach Patrol, monitors beach goers who are swimming between the flags, rescues swimmers who get into trouble, prevents drowning

Ute – Utility, Motor vehicle seating two to three passengers with a cargo tray on the back, usually with a one tonne capacity.

Salvo's – Salvation Army

Wagger – someone who skips school without permission. To wag, or ditch.

Please let me know if there are any other words you would like to have explained!